The Free Horse

Susan Carpenter Noble

BEST WISHES!

Susan Noble

Printed in the United States of America

First Printing September 2020

ISBN 978-1-64999-068-6 Paperback

Published by: Book Services
                www.BookServices.us

Contents

Dedication v

Acknowledgments. vii

1. Savannah 1

2. Grass Stains 7

3. A Visit from the Chiropractor 15

4. Sword Play 21

5. The Saddle 29

6. Emma 35

7. Unbearable 41

8. A Piece of My Heart 47

9. The Water Fight 53

10. Magnetized 59

11. Dandelions 63

12. Violet 69

13. The Rodeo 75

14. Bucking and Barrels 81

15. Send in the Clowns 87

16. This Cowgirl Won't Quit 91

17. The Pecking Order 99

18. Who's the Leader? 105

19. Feelings. 111
20. Transformation 115
21. Found Out 121
22. Ring Sour. 127
23. Emma and Skittles 131
24. Traffic Jam 137
25. Patterns. 145
26. Horse for Sale?. 153
27. Wasps 159
28. She Likes Me 167
29. And the Winner is... 173
30. For All Concerned 177
About the Author 183

Dedication

To **Cameron Elder**, who, as a little girl, got a mare from a "horse rescue" program. The mare turned out to be angry, with a proclivity for kicking and bucking. It was Cameron's efforts to rehabilitate her mare that inspired this novel. Her story is, of course, different from Meghan's in this work of fiction. Cameron ran for—and won—the title of Ute Mountain Roundup Rodeo Princess. In fact, that's Cameron on the cover of this book. She and her mare went on to have a successful horse show career. Before going off to university, Cameron sold her outgrown mare to another young rider, giving the mare a good future. I am proud of Cameron Elder and others like her who have the patience, courage, and love to save frightened, hurting animals, bring them back to good health, and then retrain them to be "good citizens."

And to **Andrea Wark** for showing me how capable, hard-working, and successful a determined young woman can be, no matter what life throws at her.

The Free Horse

Acknowledgments

Thank you to Shauna Wark for contributing to the accuracy of the details about Down syndrome and for sharing what it's like to have a Down syndrome over-achiever in the family!

Thank you to Clayton Sullwood, D.C. and Petra Sullwood, D.C. of Equus Chiropractic (Mancos, CO); and to Iris Davidson, D.C., Durango Animal Chiropractor (Durango, CO), for keeping me straight (pun intended) regarding equine chiropractic as described in this novel.

Thank you to my family for your encouragement and humor.

Thank you to Betsy Hoyt and Michael Feinberg for continuing to believe in Meghan and her adventures.

And thank you, dear reader, for coming along for the ride!

Chapter 1
Savannah

I couldn't get any air into my lungs, which was scary because, as someone with twelve years' experience breathing, I really should be better at it than this. Gasping for air, I looked up in time to see Xender catch my horse. Well, that was good at least.

On my next gasp, I felt a tiny amount of air actually going where it was supposed to. Trying again, I was rewarded with a few molecules more. Relief flowed in with the oxygen, and I relaxed a bit, which made the breathing thing a little easier. After what seemed like way too long a time, I finally began breathing almost like a normal human being again.

"You really need to stop doing that," Xender said as he handed me my reins. He turned away to get back on his own horse before adding, "I saw how your mom freaked out the last time you fell off. If you keep doing that, she's not going to let you keep riding."

"Thanks for your wonderful advice," I wheezed with as much sarcasm as possible, which under the circumstances, wasn't much.

"Need a hand up?" he asked, hesitating before he put his foot into his own stirrup.

He may have been my best friend, but I wasn't about to give him an opportunity to brag, "I had to help Meghan up after she got dumped *again.*"

"No," I grumped. "I can get back on her myself." Of course, that meant I would first have to get up off the ground. Which I did. Slowly. Everything seemed to be working okay. Other than getting the wind knocked out of me, I didn't seem to have any major damage.

My pretty little palomino mare was taking advantage of her opportunity by nibbling at the tender early-summer grass that grew in clumps around the sagebrush. Gently, I pulled on the reins, getting her away from her snack. I began bending her in circles, making sure she was responding to the reins before I climbed back on her.

"At least you're getting better at falling," Xender remarked.

"Better?" I asked suspiciously.

"Yeah, better. You're not sticking your arms out anymore. Grandpa will be proud of you 'cause he was starting to worry you'd break your arm or your collar bone if you didn't stop that."

Chapter 1 - Savannah

"Uh huh. I'm sure Ben will be positively thrilled that all I'm doing now is getting the wind knocked out of me."

"Aww, you just had a little bad luck this time. She dumped you going uphill where you couldn't roll. You wouldn't have hit so hard if you'd been able to roll. You'll do better next time."

"Next time. There's a comforting thought." In the two weeks I'd owned Savannah, I'd had the wind knocked out of me twice, not including today, and I'd been dumped a total of five times. No, six. Wait— seven. Definitely seven.

"In case you actually care, you've got some sticks or something stuck in your hair," Xender told me.

I reached back and picked out a few bits of twig. There was probably more in my dark brown, tangled ponytail, but at the moment, I needed to be concentrating on my horse.

"That's what you get for letting someone give you a free horse," Xender said.

"They didn't give her to me. They gave her to my parents. My parents gave her to me," I clarified. "And you know that my parents don't know anything about horses. Dad still calls her a him."

After bending the little mare a few more times, I walked around to her other side and started turning her that way.

"You were pretty excited to get her as I remember it."

"Of course I was. With Rowdy hurt, I didn't have a horse to ride."

I loved Rowdy. He was Ol' Ben's oldest ranch horse, the horse I'd learned to ride on when we had moved to the little town of Dolores, Colorado nearly three years ago. "I mean, your Grandpa let me ride Freckles a few times, which was really fun, but it's not like he's going to let me keep riding one of his training horses. So what was I supposed to do when Savannah showed up? Tell Mom and Dad that I didn't want a horse of my own?"

"I would have," Xender said. "At least I'd have told them I didn't want this one."

"Aww, c'mon. Look at her! She's beautiful."

Unlike when she first arrived, her golden coat now gleamed in the sun, and her white mane and tail shone like silk.

"Okay, so the brushing and all the good feed she's getting are making her look pretty, but Meghan, what good is *pretty* without brains and a good attitude?"

"She's got brains," I asserted.

"Yeah, I suppose she does. Just look at all the different ways she's figured out how to dump you."

"You just wait! She's going to turn out to be a good horse," I told him.

"I *am* waiting. I'm waiting for you to get back on her," he said.

"I will. As soon I'm sure she's listening." I continued turning her in circles. "I wish she would start putting some weight on. She's so narrow I don't have much to wrap my legs around."

"Grandpa said she probably won't start gaining weight 'til we can put her out with the herd. She's so mad about being locked up by herself that she never stops fretting and trying to get to the other horses."

"Her Coggins test results should be back any day now. That's the last thing we're waiting on from the veterinarian. As soon as we get it and know for *sure* she doesn't have Equine Infectious Anemia"—I was proud that I could finally remember that term—"she can go out. Maybe that will help calm her down," I added hopefully.

I finished bending her and then walked back around to the side where I'd started. Taking a deep breath, I gathered up my reins, stuck my foot into the stirrup, and stepped up into the saddle. Slowly I loosened the reins, releasing her head, and waited to see what would happen.

The Free Horse

Chapter 2
Grass Stains

"Quit being a passenger," Xender reminded me, sounding a whole lot like his grandpa. "Keep her busy; get her mind on you! Don't wait for her to decide what *she's* going to do to *you*. Put her to work! C'mon, Meghan Callahan, you're a better rider than that."

I wasn't feeling much like a good rider. What I was feeling was fear. Until two weeks ago, that was something I'd never before felt on horseback. And I didn't like it.

After urging Savannah forward, I kept her busy by turning her, doing circles and other patterns around the bushes, rocks, and trees as we continued our ride. Eventually we returned to the barn—with no more wrecks.

Xender's grandpa drove up in his pickup while I was unsaddling Savannah. I left her tied to the hitching rack outside the barn while I carried the saddle and bridle into the tack room to put them away.

"How was yer ride, Meghan?" Ben's voice drifted in from the other end of the barn as he carried a bag of horse feed in through the far door.

"She's doing a little better every day," I told him, which was at least partially true. I looked back at Xender, who was walking into the barn with his own saddle. He winked at me and didn't bring up the matter of my getting dumped.

"Glad to hear it," Ben said. "Did ya work her in the round pen before ya climbed on her today?"

"Yes, sir! And she's getting a lot better about that! It doesn't take nearly as long to get her to join up with me as it used to. She was following me around in less than five minutes. She's letting me pick up her feet a little easier too. But she still doesn't like to have her ears touched."

"Hmm," was all Ben said before returning to his truck for another sack of grain.

I went back out to the hitching rack to finish caring for my mare. Pulling a rubber currycomb out of the wire basket that was nailed on the side of the barn, I went to work currying her to remove the sweat that had already dried in the warmth of the June sunshine. As usual, I stayed alert, watching the mare's body language for signs that she was about to kick. A couple of times, while I rubbed the currycomb in a circle along her back, Savannah flattened her ears and cocked a hind foot, but she never actually struck out at me. That was an improvement.

8

Chapter 2 - Grass Stains

Xender's buckskin-colored horse, Scout, grazed twenty feet away on a patch of grass. His coat was a golden brown, a few shades darker than Savannah's. But instead of a white mane and tail like hers, his were black, the same color as his legs. While Scout enjoyed a few bites of grass, Xender pulled off his helmet, grabbed the end of a hose and doused his own short blonde hair with water.

"You're so lucky. I wish I could take my helmet off."

"If your parents see you anywhere near that horse without your brain box on, they'll ground you for a month."

After currying, I walked back to the wire basket to trade the curry comb for a brush. A blast of water hit me square in the back. It was so cold it nearly took my breath away. Again.

Xender was laughing. "That feel better?" he asked as he turned the hose away.

It did, actually, very cooling. Not that I was going to admit it. Instead I shot him a look that promised future paybacks.

Savannah was glaring at me warily. She had jumped when the water hit me, even though none of it had touched her. I eased up to her and used the brush gently on her shoulder. When she seemed to relax a little, I tried to brush near the top of her neck, where the sweat had probably made the base of her ears itchy. As usual, Savannah shook her head violently. With patience, I was finally able to brush her gently just a few inches *away* from her ears, but that was as close as I could get.

9

Xender, who had been watching while he curried his own horse, commented, "Looks as if she's still being stupid about her ears."

"She's not stupid," I argued. "She's just sensitive."

"She is that," Ben said from the shade of the barn door.

"You know," I said, "the way she acts kind of reminds me of how I felt last winter when I got sinusitis and had a really bad headache with it. Really bad. I mean, like, my eyelashes even hurt."

Ben chuckled at that, and added, "I know jes' what you mean, Meghan. I had one of those headaches my own self once."

"I remember sitting at the kitchen table, trying to keep up on homework," I continued. "Mom walked past me and put her hand on my shoulder, and I must have jumped a foot out of the chair. I wanted to scream at her. Everything hurt, and I didn't want anyone touching me. Well, that's how it seems Savannah feels."

Ben looked her over and observed, "Her nose an' eyes are clear. I don't see any kinda drainage from sinus problems."

"Me either," I agreed. "But there are other reasons for being touchy, aren't there? Then there's the way she always wants to kick at me when I curry along her back, and the way she lopes. I know it sounds crazy, but do you think her back is hurt?"

"Could be," Ben said. "How *does* she feel when you're ridin' her, Meghan? When you compare her to the other horses you've ridden?"

"Well, her trot is a lot bumpier than either Rowdy or Freckles. She doesn't feel lame or anything, but it feels like she's slapping her feet into the dirt almost as if she's afraid she's going to miss the ground."

"How 'bout her canter?" Ben asked.

"I haven't been able to get her to canter very much. In fact," I admitted, "I haven't even tried unless you're around."

"That's probably a wise choice. She does seem inclined to want to buck a little when she's lopin'," Ben acknowledged. "Is she gettin' any softer in the bridle?"

"Maybe a little. But she's nowhere near as easy to turn as Freckles or Rowdy. And she doesn't seem to want to drop her head down very willingly. I can get her to do it, but she's not very happy about it."

"Hmm," Ben said again.

"One more thing about her canter, except I'm not sure how to explain it." I hesitated, trying to find the right words. "It almost feels as if her front end and her back end aren't actually connected. It's really weird."

"You might be onto somethin' here, Meghan." Ben looked thoughtful for a few minutes. "I've been hearin' about an equine chiropractor who's been workin' in the area. Rumor has it she's gettin' good results with the horses. I think we need to have her come work on your little mare. If you don't have any objections, I'll call and clear it with yer folks."

"Sounds good to me!" I said. But then, anything that might possibly improve Savannah's attitude sounded good to me.

Ben started to walk past Savannah and me, then stopped and turned. "How did she dump you today?"

I looked over his shoulder at Xender, who was shaking his head and mouthing the words, "I didn't tell him."

Ben must have seen my accusing look toward his grandson. He laughed. "Meghan, you didn't have grass stains on yer shirt when you showed up here this mornin'. About the only way you coulda got 'em was by partin' company with that mare in an unexpected manner."

"She spooked at a bird and then started bucking," I admitted. "Mom's going to be really upset when she finds out."

"But you're not hurt, are ya?" Ben asked.

"No. It knocked the wind out of me, but I'm fine."

"We're gonna have to get you so you're quicker about gettin' her head around to yer knee to keep her from buckin' too hard," Ben said. "That jes' takes experience. And you're sure gettin' lots of that."

As Ben moved out of earshot, Xender suggested, "Maybe you shouldn't tell your Mom you fell off today. I mean, you don't have to lie to her or anything. You just don't have to mention it. There's no reason to go worrying her any more than she already is." Xender grinned as he added, "But this might be a good time to learn how to do your own laundry."

The Free Horse

Chapter 3
A Visit from the Chiropractor

Somehow, Ben got my parents' approval for the equine chiropractor's visit.

"Give this mare a few days off," she told me as she finished. "She responded really well to the adjustment, considering how badly her spine was out of alignment, but her muscles and tendons need a little time to get used to being back where they belong."

"Okay," I said.

It bothered me a little at how relieved I felt knowing I wasn't going to have to ride Savannah for a while.

The chiropractor showed me a picture of a horse's skeleton. "Your poor little horse must have had a raging headache, as badly as she was out at the poll," she said, circling the joint where a horse's neck attaches to the skull. Then she circled more places. "Her neck was out here. Her withers," she said, circling the spine where the shoulders attached to it, "were out. And I don't know if

15

I've ever seen a horse that was torqued so badly at her S.I. joint." She circled the spot where the pelvis attaches to the spine. "S.I. stands for sacroiliac," she explained. "Now turn her out where she can move around a little, but isn't likely to play too hard or to fight with another horse."

"How about that round pen," I asked, pointing.

"Perfect," she said, as she handed me the picture of the skeleton. "And here's my business card. Call me if you or your folks have any other questions." She climbed into her truck and drove off down the lane.

I was glad to have that piece of paper to show my parents. They hadn't been very happy about having another bill to pay, especially after all the vet bills. Along with the Coggins Test, Savannah had needed all of her vaccinations and a bunch of dental work. The vet had pulled out a couple of "wolf teeth," explaining that they were extra teeth some horses grow. She said they often grow in a spot where the bit hits them, causing the horse to throw its head in pain when the rider pulls on the reins. Then the vet had to file down some sharp edges on her teeth that were preventing her from chewing her food properly. For some reason, filing a horse's teeth is called "floating" them, which seems like a weird name for it. But whatever it's called, I'm glad it was done because it's supposed to help Savannah gain weight and start feeling better.

Along with the veterinarian, we had to have the far-rier come out and work on her hooves, which had grown way too long and were cracked and splitting when we got her. By the time he got done with his nippers and file, her feet looked balanced and smooth. The farrier said her hooves were tough enough that I could probably ride her without shoes, as long as we kept them trimmed regularly and didn't let them get back in the bad shape they'd been in before. Not having to put shoes on her cut the farrier's bill by about half. That made my parents a little happier.

Then there was the problem of her registration papers. The friend of a friend who gave the mare to us dropped her off the day he was moving away. He had handed my parents a *copy* of her registration papers, not the originals.

According to the copy, her full name was "My Savannah Pearl."

Within a few days, Xender started calling her "Mean Sow Pig" instead.

"Same initials," he said, "but it fits her better."

When my parents checked with the American Quarter Horse Association about getting Savannah's registration papers transferred into my name, they found out that the last few people who had owned the mare had not bothered to legally transfer her, so now my parents were having to get a bunch of paperwork done and pay a bunch of fees, just to get Savannah's original papers.

"That's some *free* horse we got," one of my parents lamented at least once a day.

Since I wasn't supposed to do anything with Savannah for a few days after the chiropractor's visit, I asked if I could bring Rowdy in from the pasture and brush him.

"Sure!" Ben said, sounding pleased. "The old horse is probably feelin' kinda left out these days. I bet he'd like some attention."

I picked up a halter and a handful of grain and started for the pasture. I'd barely taken ten steps past the gate when Rowdy saw me. After biting off a last mouthful of grass, he started ambling toward me. The large white blaze that ran down the middle of his face stood out brightly against his reddish-brown, mud-spattered coat. As soon as I whistled, he broke into a trot. I was really happy to see that he didn't appear to be limping at all! When he got to me, he gently lipped the grain out of my hand.

I slipped the halter over his head and started toward the gate. "Hey, ol' man, it's good to see you looking so happy. You don't even look lame anymore! Ben said you'd be good as new in a few weeks and he was right. I sure was scared for you the day you fell. You really tore your legs up. But look at you now—no more swelling, and your cuts and scrapes are mostly healed up. All that time we spent doctoring you and hosing your poor, swollen legs the first few days really paid off. Maybe I should hose you off today too. Look at you! What a mess. You must have found a *really* good patch of mud to roll in this time." I kept babbling to him as we went through the pasture gate and headed toward the barn. He was such a good old horse; more like an old friend. The way his ears followed me when I talked to him— Sometimes I was pretty sure he understood what I said.

With a currycomb, I was able to get the caked mud off of him. Then I spent a long time brushing him and cleaning his feet, which was actually fun. I'd almost forgotten how nice it is to work with a horse who didn't want to kick me or bite me. I wondered if I was ever going to feel this confident around Savannah.

As I was finishing with Rowdy, Ben led Freckles up to the hitching rack. Freckles was the tall sorrel three-year-old colt I had been allowed to ride on the cattle drive for the two days after Rowdy got hurt. While Ben unsaddled the big reddish-brown horse, he commented, "I was watchin' Rowdy trot in from the pasture. He looked plumb sound to me."

"Yes, sir, he did!" I agreed.

"Well, in that case, maybe you oughta put him back to work," Ben said. "Nothin' strenuous. Jes' hop up on him and take him for a little trail ride. Shucks, you don't even have to bother with a saddle or a bridle if you don't want to."

I started to untie him, but Ben said, "Now hold on a minute. Jes' 'cause you're not ridin' that Mean S—" He stopped himself and said, "...that mare of yours, doesn't mean you don't need a brain box on yer head."

I tied Rowdy back up and ran into the barn to grab my helmet. Once it was strapped in place, I led Rowdy away from the hitching rack and positioned him so that I was on the uphill side. Jumping up, I landed with my stomach across his withers and then swung my right leg over his back. It felt absolutely wonderful to be sitting on a horse I could trust!

The Free Horse

Chapter 4
Sword Play

"By golly," Ben said. You've gotten pretty good at hoppin' on bareback that way, Meghan. I think maybe now it's time for you to try swingin' up. With yer long legs, it shouldn't be too tough to do. Here, let me show you." He untied Freckles from the hitching rack and stood next to the colt's shoulder, facing the hindquarters. Grabbing a handful of the big horse's reddish-colored mane, he vaulted onto Freckles' back, landing seated just behind his withers. The colt jumped a little in surprise, but Ben stroked his neck and talked to him quietly until the young horse relaxed. He dismounted and then swung up again. Ben made it look easy, even though he was probably a full inch shorter than me, and his horse was nearly six inches taller than Rowdy. The colt didn't flinch on this second try, and Ben patted him approvingly on his neck.

Ben slid off Freckles' back and walked around to the other side just as Xender rode around the corner of the barn on his horse.

"Ya gotta teach a young horse like this to accept things from both sides of his body," Ben explained and swung up from the off side as well. Once again, the colt seemed a little startled, but just as before, Ben was able to soothe him.

"Hey, I want to try that too," Xender said, unsaddling Scout.

While Xender carried his saddle into the barn, I stepped up next to Rowdy's shoulder, grabbed a handful of mane, and attempted to swing my leg up over his back. All I managed to do, though, was to bounce my leg off of his side before slithering back to the ground.

Unlike Ben's young horse, Rowdy never even flinched, but stood patiently while I continued to practice.

"Bend yer knees a little more before ya launch yerself," Ben suggested.

I did and this time I managed to get my foot just over Rowdy's back. I hung there for a few seconds before I fell off.

"You're gettin' closer," Ben said.

Xender walked out of the barn as I hit the dirt. He laughed. That made me even more determined. I bent my knees and threw my leg up as high as I could. This time I got my entire lower leg over Rowdy's back, and by pulling and squirming, I was able to climb all the way up on him!

"All right!" said Ben.

"Watch this," said Xender and swung up onto Scout's back as easily as Ben had on Freckles.

"Let's see you both try it from the other side," Ben suggested. Xender and I each dismounted and walked to the horses' right shoulders.

"You first, Meghan," Xender said.

I jumped up, but didn't quite make it. In fact I didn't make it 'til the fifth try. "It's harder on this side," I said.

"That's 'cause you're used to gettin' on from the horse's left side. So it jes' don't feel natural to do things from the right. But if we want our horses to be athletic in both directions, we've got to make ourselves be that way too," Ben said. He turned toward Xender. "Now you try it."

Xender took two tries before he made it.

"Looks to me like you both need to work on bein' ambidextrous," Ben said.

"Being what?" Xender asked.

"Ambidextrous. Doin' things from both sides," Ben explained. "Xender, why don't you go along with Meghan. She's gonna take Rowdy for a little trail ride. And yer horse could use a nice mental break after you worked him so hard in the arena this mornin'."

"Sure, Grandpa," he said.

We turned our horses and started toward a trail that runs alongside the Dolores River. It was another gorgeous June day. Xender found a good spot to walk his horse into the river, and I followed him on Rowdy. Both horses stood contentedly in the water, plunging their muzzles in for a drink. A few weeks ago, the stream had been rushing and muddy with snowmelt from the high mountains north and east of us. But now the water was running clear again.

While Rowdy drank his fill, I wondered aloud, "Why *do* we always saddle the horses from their left side and put their halters on from the left and mount and dismount from the left?"

"Grandpa says it's because people used to carry long swords."

"Oh, quit clowning around."

"No, seriously, think about it. Are you left-handed or right-handed?" he asked.

"Right-handed."

"Okay then," he said, reaching up and breaking off a dead branch from a tree that extended out over the water. He snapped off the skinniest end as well as the smaller twigs that stuck off of it; then he handed me the three-foot-long stick. "Here's your sword."

I raised it up over my head as if I were about to charge into battle. "All right!" I couldn't help giggling.

"Yeah. Now, pretend you're putting your sword back into its scabbard, you know, the thing that holds the sword."

"Where is it?"

"On your belt," he said.

"Which side?"

"Figure it out," he grinned. Xender always got a smug smile on his face when he got to teach me something he had learned from his grandpa. "Where's it easier to put the sword away?"

I fumbled with my sword, experimenting.

"And if another knight attacked you," he continued, "which side could you pull it out of faster to defend yourself?"

With a total lack of grace and skill, I first tried to put it away on my right side. I quickly discovered that I had to twist my wrist into an awkward position to get that done. Finally, I realized that if I slipped it into its imaginary scabbard on the other side, I could do it easily.

"Left."

"Yep," he agreed. "Now picture yourself getting on your horse from the horse's *right* side if you had a big long sword hanging off the left side of your belt."

I ran through the steps in my head. "Um, that would be a problem."

"Why?" Xender grinned again, breaking off another dead branch and making a second sword.

"Because my sword would be between me and my horse, and I would probably stick it into my horse's flank as I got on."

"Yep," Xender said. "Do you understand now?"

"Yeah, I think so. Getting on from the left would keep my sword away from my horse."

"You got it," Xender agreed.

"But what about left-handed people? I mean, it seems as if most of the people I know are right-handed except my aunt, who always complains that everything is made wrong. But there *are* left-handed people, and some of them must've carried swords too."

"Grandpa says that when he was a boy, left-handed kids usually got their hands whacked when they tried to use them, so they grew up learning to do stuff right-handed."

"Really? That's just mean!"

Xender nodded in agreement. "Anyway, *most* people are right-handed so I guess most horses were trained to be handled from the left so they wouldn't get stabbed by their own rider. And it became a tradition. At least, that's how Grandpa explains it."

We rode up the bank out of the creek, and while Xender and I played with our swords, Scout and Rowdy ambled along at a relaxed pace, ignoring us.

"I don't think the Mean Sow Pig would put up with sword fighting," Xender said as we got back to the barn.

I wished I could have argued with him, but I knew he was right. So as soon as we both got our horses tied up, I attacked him with my sword. We battled back and forth between the barn and the pasture gate, until we were both out of breath and laughing. We might have resumed, but Jace Carlton drove his pickup truck up the lane before either one of us had decided to launch a fresh attack.

"Uh oh," Xender said. "Violet's going to be mad. There's a girl in the front seat with Jace."

The Free Horse

Chapter 5
The Saddle

There was a glare on the windshield, so I couldn't see who it was until the truck was nearly to the barn. Then I laughed at Xender. "That's Jace's mom," I said. "So I don't think your sister's world is going to end today."

"Speaking of..." Xender nodded back toward his house. Following his gaze, I saw his petite, honey blonde sister, Violet, walking casually toward the barn. As usual, her hair and makeup looked perfect, and her tight jeans and fitted shirt made her look the part of a Junior Rodeo Queen, which is what she was planning to be this summer. That's why I was totally surprised when Jace spoke first to me instead of to Violet.

"Hey, Meghan," he called as he stepped out of his truck, "we brought you something."

At that particular moment, I was walking over to untie the ever-patient Rowdy from the hitching rack where he had stood dozing in the sun through our sword fight. I stopped in my tracks at Jace's greeting. Glancing at Violet, I saw her pretty smile fade abruptly.

As Jace walked around to the back of his truck, his mom stepped out of the passenger side of the cab to greet me. "Oh, Meghan, I'm so glad you're here! I've been wanting to thank you and I finally figured out how."

"You already said thanks, Mrs. Carlton."

"What you did on the cattle drive takes more than just words for a proper thank you," Mrs. Carlton said, looking back over her shoulder to see where Jace was. I followed her gaze. He was walking toward us carrying a saddle. "So I talked to Ben and found out you've been borrowing a saddle from him. Well, since my oldest daughter moved away and gave up riding, I decided there was no point in keeping this saddle around collecting dust. I want you to have it."

I looked at her in disbelief. But Jace walked up to me and handed me the saddle, which was a little heavier than the one I was used to, so instead of saying "thanks," which I was too tongue-tied to say anyway, I just sort of went, "Oomph!"

Jace turned away and walked over to Violet, who was instantly all smiles again.

Mrs. Carlton somehow looked happy and anxious at the same time. "Well? What do you think? Do you like it?" she asked.ß

"It's— it's absolutely gorgeous!"

Chapter 5 - The Saddle

"Let's have you try it and make sure it fits you!" she suggested.

"I'll go get a saddle blanket," Xender volunteered and took off for the barn.

I lugged the heavy saddle over toward the hitching rack, and by the time I got there, Xender was back, putting the blanket on Rowdy. Ben was right behind him.

Ben tipped his hat to Mrs. Carlton.

"Is it okay for me to saddle up Rowdy?" I asked Ben.

"I don't think that would hurt him one bit," Ben grinned.

While I swung the saddle up onto Rowdy's back, the adults stood behind me talking. With Xender's help, I got all of the straps adjusted and then cinched up the saddle. I couldn't believe how beautiful it was. The leather had intricate carvings of Colorado Columbine, one of my favorite flowers, at the front and back corners of the saddle skirts, as well as toward the bottom of the stirrup fenders. And there were fancy silver conchos on it where the saddle strings were attached. This saddle was a work of art!

"You'll probably need to lengthen those stirrups a few holes," Mrs. Carlton pointed out. "My daughter's tall, but not as tall as you are."

I let the stirrups down to about four inches below Rowdy's belly, which is where the stirrups on the saddle I usually rode seemed to reach.

"Go ahead," Ben said. "Tie the other end of yer lead rope back to his halter to make you some reins and then step up into that saddle."

I led Rowdy away from the hitching rack, fixed the lead rope, and mounted up. Settling my weight gently onto Rowdy's back, I looked down at the top of the saddle horn. "It's got my initials carved on it!" I blurted out.

Mrs. Carlton started laughing. "I hadn't thought about that, but— sure. We had Melissa's initials put on it when we had it made for her."

"The seat's too big for you," Ben said.

My heart sank.

"But by the time you're done growin', it's likely goin' to be exactly right," he added.

My heart soared again. "Mrs. Carlton, except for Ben teaching me how to ride, this is the nicest thing anyone has ever done for me!"

"Well, you earned it, Meghan," she said, "and my daughter has made it abundantly clear to me that she is not *ever* stepping up on a horse again, so there's no point in letting a perfectly good saddle go unused." After a hesitation, she added. "I do have one request though."

"Yes, ma'am?"

"I want you to clean it and oil it real good before you start using it. It has been sitting in our barn drying up and gathering dust for over two years now.

Then I expect you to keep it cleaned and cared for the way a quality saddle deserves. It'll last you a lifetime if you do."

"Oh, I will!" I promised.

"I figured you would," Mrs. Carlton said, "or I wouldn't have entrusted it to you." She looked around. "Now where did my son wander off to?"

"He's sittin' in the shade on the front steps with my granddaughter. I've been keepin' an eye on 'em," Ben said.

After I turned Rowdy back into the pasture, Jace and Mrs. Carlton gave me a ride home. Usually I walked, since it's less than a quarter of a mile from Ben's barn to my house, but when they saw me pick up the saddle and start for home, they insisted on giving me a lift. Jace hoisted the saddle into the bed of the pickup, and I climbed in after it.

"Wait for me! That looks like fun," Xender yelled, running over and jumping into the back of the truck with me. We sat on the tailgate, our feet dangling over the edge.

"Hold on tight!" cautioned Mrs. Carlton.

We each grabbed the side of the truck closest to us with one hand and the edge of the tailgate with the other. But when Xender heard Mrs. Carlton tell Jace to drive slowly and miss the potholes, he jumped back out.

"It would've been a fun ride if his mother wasn't with him," he grumbled as he headed back to the barn.

But I wasn't grumbling. I didn't want my new saddle to get any scratches on it, and it might have if Jace drove out the lane the way he usually did.

Chapter 6
Emma

Sitting on the back porch, where I had just finished cleaning and oiling my new saddle, I heard Mom's car as she arrived home from the dentist office where she worked.

"She just *gave* it to you?" she asked me about ten times while we were putting away the groceries. "I can't believe anyone would just give such a beautiful saddle away. Are you sure she's not just loaning it to you?"

"Pretty sure, Mom. For one thing, she said it would last me a lifetime if I cared for it properly."

Mom still looked doubtful, but at least she finally changed the subject. "Mr. Nelson was in the office today. He asked about you."

"Who's Mr. Nelson?"

"Emily's dad. He said you were really nice to his daughter in school this past year."

"Emily?"

"You know, the little Down syndrome girl. I remember you talking about her a few times."

"Oooohhh. Emma. Yeah, she's a sweet kid."

"Emma? Oh, okay. Well anyway, her dad said you were really helpful to Emma in her science and P.E. classes."

"Those are the only two classes we were in together."

"It sounds as if you made quite an impression on her."

"Yeah, well that's probably because she was terrified of me because of my height when she first saw me. She wouldn't get anywhere near me! She stopped dead in her tracks and started pointing, saying something about an ogre."

Mom laughed.

"Actually, I was kind of irritated at first, but then I got over it. I mean, she doesn't seem to have a lot going for her in the way of social skills."

"Meghan!" Mom said sharply.

"Well, it's true. Some of the other kids make fun of her because she's different. I didn't need to be mean to her too, just because of something dumb like my height."

"She must have gotten over her fear," Mom ventured.

"I guess so. Probably when we were in science class."

"Did something happen?" she asked.

"Well, I told the teacher that I didn't want to work with a partner for the final project at the end of fall term and she said I had to. I didn't exactly hide the fact that I was not happy. Anyway, she asked if I would be willing to have Emma work with me. At first I was annoyed, but then it hit me that Emma would probably go along with whatever project I wanted and wouldn't get in the way. So I said yes."

"How was she?" asked Mom.

"Actually, she was great. She let me make all the decisions and just kind of tagged along or sat and watched. But sometimes, when she saw something she could do, or when I asked her to help with something, she would get the biggest smile on her face and would jump right in. She ended up being a good helper."

"What about P.E. class?" Mom persisted.

"Well that was spring semester, and when Emma saw me that first day of class, I guess she remembered she wasn't scared of me anymore. She started following me around like she did when we worked on the science project. She seems sort of shy. And Mom, I'm not trying to be mean, but some of the other kids don't think she can do anything."

"Neither did you at first," Mom pointed out.

"Ow. Yeah, well I got over it." I hurried on. "I mean, she's not the best athlete in the class, but neither am I. And she's really young. I mean, she's my age, but she's really small, and the way she acts and talks, sometimes you'd swear she's like six or seven years old. Anyway, if she needed some extra help to understand how a game was played or needed extra practice with something, I just tried to help her a little. That's all. It was no big deal."

"It was to Mr. Nelson," Mom said. "It's hard on a parent when they've got a child who isn't, um, the same as the other kids."

"Aren't you the one who always says, 'All kids are unique. You should be proud of your differences'?" I teased her.

"Well, you're different in lots of good ways."

"Yeah, Mom. Being a foot taller than every other kid in my class is really terrific," I replied, with no effort to keep the sarcasm out of my voice.

"Oh honey, you know what I mean. You may be taller than the other kids, but you're also blessed with a sharp mind and a healthy body. You're so fortunate." She paused. "Poor little Emma is dealing with something the rest of us will probably never understand."

I wondered about that. "What exactly is Down syndrome, Mom?"

"It's a genetic thing that affects how a person learns," she said. "They need a lot more time, more repetition, and more practice to learn things."

"That sounds like Emma," I said.

Mom went on, "A friend of mine with a Down syndrome daughter said that the wiring in her daughter's brain is just plain different. She explained it by saying it's like trying to plug an electric cord into an electric outlet that doesn't match up with it. So she has to adjust her expectations for her girl. She also said that kids and adults with Down syndrome can be a little short on social skills and have difficulty with communication."

Somehow I managed not to mention to Mom that she had yelled at me mere minutes ago when *I* had mentioned Emma's lack of social skills.

"I'm glad you accepted her for who she is," Mom said, which made me feel kind of uncomfortable.

"I wasn't very accepting at first," I admitted.

"Yes, but you changed," Mom smiled. "I'm glad. And Mr. Nelson is really grateful."

When Dad got home from work a little while later, I had to go through the whole yes-Mrs.-Carlton-really-gave-me-the-saddle routine a bunch more times.

Dad suddenly got a serious look on his face. "I sure hope free saddles aren't as expensive as free horses."

"It won't be Dad. Besides, technically, it wasn't free."

My parents both stopped and looked at me suspiciously.

"Mrs. Carlton said I *earned* it!"

The Free Horse

Chapter 7
Unbearable

Dad gave the saddle and me a ride to Ben's barn early the next morning when he left for work.

"Thanks, Dad," I said and carried the saddle into the barn. I found an empty rack in the tack room and carefully placed my saddle on it. *My* saddle. I still could hardly believe it. After one more admiring look at it, I turned, found the wheelbarrow and one of the apple pickers, and started toward the first pen.

The horses in the six pens alongside the barn were all munching on hay. Ben must have fed them and then gone back to the house for his own breakfast. These were horses that Ben had in training for other people. Freckles was the only training horse he kept out in the pasture with his own herd. I wasn't sure why that was. Anyway, I hoped Savannah would soon get to live out there too. For now, she was by herself in the round pen. And she didn't seem to like that one bit.

I let myself into the first pen and started cleaning. Ben always told me to talk to the horses when I was working around them so they would know I was there and wouldn't get startled and kick me. "Well, that was dumb of me, Frosty. I grabbed the apple picker with the broken tine. But don't you worry, girl, I'll still do a good job cleaning all this manure out of your pen. Usually when I beat Xender to the barn, I'm bright enough to get the one that's not broken, so I don't have to keep picking up the road apples that fall through. Oh well, if he's not here by the time I finish your pen, I'll go swap for the good one."

I traded, because not only was he not at the barn before I started cleaning the second pen, but I finished all six of them and was cleaning the round pen where Savannah lived before he showed up.

"I overslept," he yawned. "Sorry."

"You don't actually look sorry."

Xender grinned. "I'm not. Sleeping in once in a while is really nice."

"I wouldn't know."

He walked over and leaned on the round pen fence. "Hey, what's wrong with your horse?"

I stopped cleaning her pen and looked at her carefully. "Nothing that I know of. Why?"

"She didn't lay her ears back at me when I leaned on the fence. I think that's a first."

I watched her eating her hay. "You know what? She hasn't threatened to kick me once this morning. So far."

"Wow," Xender said.

"Wow is right."

"You're not supposed to ride her 'til tomorrow, are you?" he asked.

"Yeah. She's supposed to get one more day off."

"Maybe Grandpa will let you saddle up Rowdy again today."

"I hope so." I looked out toward the pasture just in time to see Rowdy lie down. "He must have heard you. I guess he's going to catch a quick nap so he's rested up for our ride," I joked while I pushed the wheelbarrow out the round pen gate.

Xender closed it behind me. Then he laughed. "Did I ever tell you about the time Rowdy walked into the river and lay down while I was on his back? I was only four or five years old at the time. It was a really hot day so he just decided to cool us both off."

I started laughing too, but then I stopped. "Xender, something's wrong! Rowdy just stood up again and look at him!"

We both watched the old horse as he walked or, more accurately, staggered, across the field, looking as if he were about to fall down.

"Get a halter, Meghan, and I'll go find Grandpa," Xender shouted over his shoulder as he bolted toward the house.

I ran into the barn, my heart pounding in fear. After grabbing a halter and lead rope, I raced back out to the pasture gate, reaching it just ahead of Xender and Ben. I fumbled with the gate latch, finally got it open, and shot through.

"Meghan!" Ben's normally quiet voice roared, "Get back here!"

The tone of his voice stopped me in my tracks. More quietly, he ordered, "Give me the halter, then stay here. Don't either one of you follow me."

"But Grandpa—"

Ben tore his gaze away from Rowdy long enough to look us both right in the eyes and then repeated, "Stay here."

Ben walked toward the old horse, talking quietly, soothingly, "Well Rowdy, you old rascal, you surely do know how to get a guy's attention. What's goin' on, ol' fella? You not feelin' so good? Let's see if we can get this figured out and try to get ya some help..." Ben's words faded as he got farther away from us.

Less than twenty feet separated the man from the horse, when Rowdy suddenly reared straight up in the air and fell over. Legs thrashing, he scrambled back to his feet, where he stood, spraddle-legged and visibly shaking. Seconds later, his knees buckled and he crashed to the ground again. His legs twitched several times, but he didn't try to stand. Ben knelt down next to his head and stroked the old horse's neck.

At the same exact second, without saying a word, Xender and I both took off at a run across the pasture. We slowed in unison as we approached the old man and the horse.

"He's gone, kids," Ben whispered. "Come say yer good-byes if you want to." Ben stood up and walked off a few yards, wiping his shirtsleeve across his eyes.

Xender threw himself down on Rowdy's neck, burying his face in Rowdy's thick black mane.

I walked over more slowly, looking at the sweet old horse who had taught me so much. His mouth was slightly open and his tongue lolled out on the ground. And his eyes! His eyes were still open but they looked really freaky—cloudy and glazed over. They didn't look like his eyes at all. I understood then why Ben had said what he said. The body on the ground may have had the same coloring as Rowdy and the same blaze as Rowdy, but it wasn't Rowdy. Not anymore. Rowdy was truly gone.

I knelt down next to him and gently rubbed the white blaze on his face. And I cried. I cried as I had never cried before.

The Free Horse

Chapter 8
A Piece of My Heart

I overslept the next morning. Images of Rowdy had been running through my brain all night, keeping me upset and awake. It was after 3:00 in the morning the last time I remembered seeing the clock next to my bed.

By the time I got to the barn, Ol' Ben was already out in the arena riding one of his training horses. Xender was nowhere to be seen. I got the wheelbarrow and apple picker, the one with all its tines, and started for the pens, averting my eyes from the pasture. I did not want to look in that direction, knowing Rowdy wouldn't be there.

To my surprise, the pens had already been cleaned. In fact, they'd been cleaned long enough that most of them already had a fresh pile or two of manure in them. I scooped each pile out before heading over to the round pen to clean it.

Savannah looked at me when I pushed the wheel-barrow through the gate, but she didn't look like she wanted to kick me. She didn't act even slightly annoyed.

A few minutes later, as I was maneuvering the wheelbarrow back out the gate, Ben walked by on his way to the barn from the arena. He was leading one of his two-year-old training horses. "This little horse is comin' along real well," Ben said, "thanks to Rowdy."

I looked up in surprise, not knowing what to say. So I didn't say anything. And that was okay because Ben seemed to be in a chatty mood.

"When Rowdy was a colt— Did you know I raised him from a baby? Anyway, when he was two years old and I started ridin' him, he showed so much talent workin' cows that I tried to push him along too fast. He was a smart horse and he wouldn't take bein' pushed. I wasn't near as smart as him, so he had to stuff my head in the dirt a few times to get his point across."

"Rowdy?!"

"Oh, yeah. That horse could buck when he was young. He never bucked when I first started ridin' him, but when I got stupid and started tryin' to crowd him too fast in his trainin', that horse would positively explode. He left me sittin' in the dirt considerin' the error of my ways quite a few times before I finally got the message. I credit Rowdy for transformin' me from a pig-headed know-it-all into a horseman."

"But didn't you win a bunch of state champion-ships on him when he was young?" I asked.

Chapter 8 - A Piece of My Heart

"Not when he was young, though he could have if I hadn't been so slow to catch on. It wasn't 'til Rowdy got *me* trained that we did any good in the show pen. He won the state in Cutting when he was six and then again when he turned seven. The next year, he won in Working Cowhorse. That was the year I was finally able to quit workin' my other job and go to trainin' horses full time." Ben smiled. "That old horse made a trainer out of me. Well, him and a couple of other ol' horsemen who helped me along."

"Ben," I asked, feeling my eyes well up with tears, "what happened to him yesterday?"

Ben sighed. "That big old heart of his gave out, Meghan. He had himself a heart attack. The pain from it was why he reared up and fell over the way he did. He tried to fight it. That's why he got back up. But then he stood there all shakin', and the look in his eyes changed. It was time for him to go and he was ready."

I felt the tears rolling down my face. "I wasn't ready."

Ben put his hand on my shoulder. "He hasn't really left you, Meghan. You'll always carry somethin' of that horse in yer heart. And what you learned from him is goin' to help every single horse you get on from here on out. Includin' that little yellow mare standin' behind you. Now, how about if you go dump all the road apples you've scraped up this mornin'? Then you can start usin' what he taught you on yer mare."

Ben turned away to take his colt over to the hitching rack. Before he'd gone two steps, I blurted out the agonizing thought that had kept me from getting to sleep last night. "Ben, did I kill Rowdy by riding him the day before?"

He stopped and turned back toward me. "Whatever put a foolish thought like that in yer head? Of course, you didn't kill him. You made his last day here on God's earth special for him. He always looked happiest when he was packin' one of you kids around."

I was suddenly crying even harder, but this time they were tears of relief.

"Besides," Ben added, "yesterday mornin' when I came down to feed the penned horses, Rowdy was racin' around the pasture buckin' and playin' like a colt. He was happy, right up to the end. Truth to tell, I envy the ol' boy that."

"Thank you, Ben," I blubbered.

"Don't thank me. It was the horse that done it," he said. "If you want to thank Rowdy, well, you can do that by applyin' what he taught you. That'd be the best way to honor his memory. So now, soon as you get done cryin', finish yer chores, and get yer mare brushed, we can get to work."

By the time I led Savannah up to the hitching rack, my face was nearly dry, and I was feeling a renewed sense of determination.

"Look at her, Ben, she's not trying to kick when I curry her back!"

"How is she with her ears?"

I eased up to the top of her neck with the brush, but when I touched it near her ears, she jerked away.

"Keep doin' that, real gentle like," Ben said. "It looked to me more like she reacted from habit, not pain."

I continued brushing gently around her ears and finally, she stood mostly still for it.

"She's got some bad habits that you're gonna have to overcome with pure, old-fashioned patience and persistence."

I untied Savannah and led her back to the round pen, where I started doing some ground work. In less time than ever, she was actually paying attention to me, with one ear cocked toward me all the time while she trotted a big circle around me.

"She's warmed up enough, Meghan," Ben hollered from over by the barn, where he was trimming the long hair off one of his training horse's legs with electric clippers. "Make her lope for a while."

Savannah had never seemed to like loping in the round pen. As usual, it took me a while to get her to go from a trot to a canter. She only went a few strides before breaking back into a trot again.

"Send her!" Ben shouted.

I encouraged her forward again by snapping my lunge whip behind her. She stepped into a canter and continued around the pen one-and-a-half times before breaking back to a trot. I snapped the whip again and she loped off right away.

"Quit lettin' her break gait, Meghan," Ben commanded. "Watch her. And send her forward *before* she drops to a trot."

I studied the mare carefully and realized I could see from her body language when she was about to slack off. If I just wiggled the lunge whip behind her when she showed signs of wanting to trot, she would continue loping. Before long, she was maintaining a steady canter around the pen.

"Now stop her when *you* want, not when she decides," Ben hollered. "Then let her air up before you send her back in the other direction."

I called, "Whoa," and took a step backward. Savannah stopped, looked at me, and walked right up to me. I stroked her on the neck and then slowly worked my way up toward her ears. She flinched a little, but she let me rub very gently around the base of one and then the other.

"Who is that horse and what have you done with Mean Sow Pig?" Xender mocked me.

Chapter 9
The Water Fight

I was so focused on my horse that I hadn't even seen Xender show up.

"She's sure doing better, isn't she?" I asked happily.

"Don't get overconfident. She may be doing better this second, but old habits die hard."

"Habits like oversleeping?" I asked. "This is two days in a row."

"What do you mean, oversleeping? Who do you think was out here at the crack of dawn cleaning the pens by himself? You're the lazy slug that didn't show up at a decent time."

"Yeah, I kinda did oversleep," I admitted. "Sorry."

"It's okay," he said unexpectedly.

"I couldn't get to sleep last night for an awful long time," I told him.

"Yeah. I know what you mean. I think I was awake most of the night too." Xender suddenly looked a little sheepish. "I went back up to the house after chores this morning, ate some breakfast, and fell asleep on the couch."

He stood with his hands shoved in his pockets, kicking the dirt with the toe of his boots. We were both silent, lost in our thoughts. I wondered if his insides felt as twisted up as mine still did.

"Xender!" his grandpa shouted. "Can you come give me a hand?"

Xender jogged off to where Ben was working with the colt and the clippers while I sent Savannah back to the round pen fence to work the other direction.

"Let's don't hurry that little mare," Ben said when I'd finished in the round pen and led her to the hitching rack. "I think she could use one more day of not ridin'. You had a good session of ground work with her jes' now and she's got plenty to think about. So how about you lead her over to that patch of grass and let her graze for ten minutes. We gotta introduce her to fresh grass a little at a time before we put her out in the pasture with the herd. Otherwise, she might colic. If you start today on the grass, then tomorrow you can give her as much as twenty minutes."

I walked Savannah toward a patch of thick grass.

Ben called after me, "When you get done, come find me. I've got some work for ya."

Chapter 9 - The Water Fight

Ben's idea of "work" was that I should ride his training horse Freckles!

Riding Freckles *did* involve some serious work, since I needed to get my new saddle all the way up onto the back of this big horse. But I got it done and led him out to where Ben was working with another young horse.

"Get on him and walk him around the arena a couple of times," Ben said, "once in each direction. Let him look things over before you ask him to go to work."

The big red colt had a huge, ground-covering stride, and we were done with that in no time.

"Now bring him to the center and curl him around to the right a few times and then back to the left a couple more."

I started to do as Ben said and almost immediately heard his quiet, but very serious voice telling me, "Careful there, Meghan, you're bein' a shade heavy-handed."

I was surprised because I felt that I had barely started to ask the horse to turn.

"Jes' lift yer hand real quiet-like and sorta melt into his mouth this time."

Freckles responded to the light touch immediately, dropping his head down and around toward the side.

"That's better," Ben said, "but you can probably be lighter still. This colt wants to be soft. So you need to let him. Just kinda suggest what you want. If he does it, leave him be. If he doesn't respond, then you can get a little more firm with him."

The whole time I rode, reminders kept coming from Ben—and Freckles—to lighten my four aids. "You learned from ridin' Rowdy that you can communicate with yer horse usin' four parts of yer body, Meghan. What are they?"

"My hands, my legs, my voice, and..." I hesitated, searching my brain for the fourth one. "My weight!" I added triumphantly.

"That's right," Ben said. "Now you need to refine how you use 'em. Remember, when you want yer horse to do somethin', you need to ask him in a way that makes sense to him. You need to think about things from the horse's point of view. When he understands and does somethin' the way you want, you reward him by leavin' him alone. Then the next time you ask, ask him even softer. Pretty quick, he'll be listenin' to ya so well, you'll start feelin' like he's readin' yer mind."

Over the next forty-five minutes, I began to understand what Ben meant. I felt as if I was actually a partner with the colt: I was thrilled at how lightly I could use my hands and still get the desired response from him.

"Now go put Freckles back out in the pasture and you can spend some time thinkin' about what you just learnt while you're cleanin' all the horse troughs," Ben said.

It didn't take long before I was sweating as I scrubbed away on one of the troughs, cleaning out the algae that turns the sides of the tank green during the warm weather. I was focusing so hard on what Ben and Freckles had taught me that morning that I didn't notice Xender sneaking up behind me until the water from the bucket he was carrying splashed across my back. I spun around with my hose and soaked him until he got too far away for the spray to reach him.

The horses in the pens near me all threw their heads up in the air and jumped away from our water fight. Out of the corner of my eye, I saw that Ben had stopped his horse in the arena and was watching us, so I quickly shut down the spray of water and busily went back to scrubbing.

"Hey, you two!" Ben shouted.

"Yes, sir?" Xender and I responded a little quietly, but practically in stereo.

"If you two are going to start somethin' like that, make sure you finish it."

Xender and I exchanged surprised looks.

Ben chuckled and continued, "You did just enough to startle those horses, but not enough to let 'em know it's okay. Keep that water fight goin' where they can see ya, but so's they know it doesn't actually involve them. Oh, and not so close that any of 'em can stomp or kick ya."

Gleefully, Xender and I resumed our fight. Within minutes, we were both drenched and the horses were either watching us or ignoring us. But they were no longer afraid.

"That's better," Ben said as he rode past. "See if you can do that again in a day or two. I like for my trainin' horses to be used to all kinds of activity before they leave here. That was a good lesson for 'em."

I giggled and went back to scrubbing and filling the troughs. Thoughts about our fun water fight were soon replaced by thoughts about all I had learned riding Freckles, and then about how much better Savannah had done today. I hoped I would be able to use everything I was learning to help her become a better horse. And that made me think about Rowdy.

I started crying all over again. I knew Ben was right: I'd always carry Rowdy in my heart. But I loved that horse and it hurt terribly to have lost him so suddenly. I started to feel guilty that I was having such a fun day just a day after Rowdy had died, and that made me cry even harder.

I looked up just as Xender came around the corner. He took one look at my face and turned away. As he did, he reached up and rubbed the back of his hand across his eyes.

I guess I wasn't the only one who was still hurting.

Chapter 10
Magnetized

"Look how much better Savannah's doing with her ears," I bragged as I gently brushed them. "She only flinched a tiny bit when I started, and now she's letting me brush around them without minding!"

"She sure does seem a lot less fretful," Ben agreed. "Finish brushin' her and then saddle her up before you start yer groundwork, Meghan."

It was a lot easier getting the saddle up on little Savannah's back than it had been on Freckles, and we were soon ready to go.

"Take her out to the round pen and work her like ya did yesterday," Ben said. "I'll finish gettin' my horse ready and be out there directly."

Savannah was much more consistent about cantering this time. That was probably because I was better at reading her body language, so she didn't have as many opportunities to be lazy as she did before.

"That's enough groundwork," Ben said as he led his training horse past the round pen. "It's time for you to get back on her. Slip her bridle on her head and bring her over to the arena."

Bridling had never been easy because she was so squirrelly about her ears. But this time I was able to put it on without too much difficulty.

"Well, that looked better," Ben called.

"Yeah," I smiled fleetingly. Except then I started thinking about the fact that I was about to get on her again. My heart started pounding and my palms suddenly felt sweaty. Making myself follow Ben's directions, I led her to the arena and closed the gate behind me.

"Bring her into the middle of the pen and step up on her, Meghan. She's probably gonna be just fine. In fact, you need to expect her to be good." Ben continued in his calmest, most reassuring voice, "Be ready, just in case. But stay real calm and quiet with her, 'cause she will feel it if you get nervous and that'll make *her* nervous."

My heart still racing, I took a deep breath and reminded myself how much better she was doing with her ears *and* her groundwork *and* picking up her feet *and* having her back curried. This was going to be totally great, I told myself. I took a couple of deep breaths, put my foot in the stirrup, and swung up into the saddle.

"Don't sit there too long, Meghan. Get her attention on you," Ben reminded me.

I urged Savannah forward, bending her at the same time.

"Remember what you learned yesterday, Meghan. Melt into her mouth real soft-like. Give her a chance to be good."

I focused on using my hands even more gently as I asked for the turns.

"Don't forget to use yer legs. If she's not listenin' to yer hands, use yer legs to reinforce what yer hands are tellin' her. Remember the rule, Meghan: ask her nicely fer what you want. If she's good, leave her alone. If she doesn't do as she's asked, then *tell* her by using yer legs harder while you stay as soft as you can with yer hands. If she still isn't listenin', then *make* her listen with yer legs. She gets three chances—ask, tell, make —but she *only* gets three. Any more than that and you're jes' naggin' her, which means she's not learnin' anything other than how to act spoiled."

Soon Savannah was walking and trotting circles all around the arena. I concentrated on keeping my hands as light as I could, so that Ben wouldn't have to keep reminding me. But every time we trotted past the arena gate, Savannah would pull toward it and slow down as if she wanted to go out.

"Looks like she's magnetized to that gate," Ben said. "Keep yer hands soft as you come around the corner toward it next time, and use yer legs to prevent her from leanin' on yer hands."

"How do you mean?" I asked.

"As soon as she leans toward the gate, reach forward with yer outside stirrup and kick her with the side of yer foot on her shoulder. But sit back when you do, 'cause she may not respond favorably the first time you try it."

As we came around the corner, she started pulling toward the gate again. I tapped her with my foot, but got no response.

"Meghan, get serious with yer foot!" Ben called.

"I don't want to hurt her," I said out loud. *Or get bucked off,* I thought to myself.

"Do you actually think you can hurt her with yer foot like that? Think about it, Meghan. When one horse tells another horse to get out of its way, what does he do? He lays his ears back as a warning, then kicks or bites him if he doesn't get the message. You are just speakin' to yer mare in a language she understands. You're warnin' her not to go to the gate with yer soft hands. If she ignores you, you're treatin' her jes' like another horse would. If you're fair to her like that, she'll start listenin' to you. And that'll make life easier for her *and* you."

When she leaned toward the gate the next time around, I kicked her with my foot on her shoulder as Ben had instructed. She jumped a little, away from my foot. Then she bucked.

Chapter 11
Dandelions

I stayed on!

"Bend her around and kick her like you mean it with that same foot!" Ben shouted. "She is *not* allowed to smart off at you like that. You make that clear to her!"

I did as he told me and soon Savannah was turning in a tight circle so fast that I was getting dizzy. I grabbed the saddle horn with one hand and kept kicking.

"Okay, that's enough," Ben said. "Now just jog her back around the arena as if nothin' happened. But if she leans toward the gate on the next pass, you kick her in the shoulder again, every bit as hard as you did that last time. Just remember to keep yer hands soft and light. Otherwise, you're not teachin' her anything."

Savannah leaned again and I kicked again. Once more, she bucked and once more, I bent her around and kicked her with my inside foot.

"Good. You handled that jes' right," Ben said. "Ride her on around again."

This time when she leaned and I kicked, she didn't try to buck. The next time around, she didn't pull toward the gate at all, but listened instead to my quiet hands.

"She's startin' to understand," Ben said. "Stop her at the other end of the arena, pet her, and let her stand still for a few minutes so she can think about it and rest up a little. She's earned it." He chuckled. "So have you."

"Ben? Are you sure I'm not hurting her when I kick her like that?" I asked.

"Well, to be honest, I don't guess gettin' kicked is the best feelin' in the world, Meghan, but if you don't do this fer yer mare, she's not goin' to learn to behave herself. And if she doesn't learn to behave, she's not gonna be able to find a good home when you outgrow her. Sometimes you have to get tough on a horse that's been allowed to develop bad manners. In the long run, you're helpin' her out. And as long as you're fair by rewardin' her when she's good, she will accept correction from you, just like she accepts it from other horses."

While I petted Savannah and told her in my most soothing voice what a good girl she was being, Ol' Ben worked his training horse.

Ben's words echoed in my head: *when you outgrow her.* How soon would that be? Would I love her as much by then as I had loved Rowdy? Would I have to

64

part with her just because I was too tall? And would it hurt as badly as saying goodbye to Rowdy?

Ben stopped to rest his training horse. "Turn yer mare around and try it in the other direction," he said. And remember, the wires don't hardly cross from the left side of a horse's brain to the right side, so she's probably goin' to try the same stunt this way."

Just as Ben had predicted, Savannah tried pulling toward the gate, and we had to repeat the process. But she was soon listening to me in that direction too.

"Go let her stand in the middle of the arena and air up while I work this filly some more," Ben said, as soon as Savannah was being good.

When it was our turn again, Savannah and I trotted around the arena, doing circles and reverses and passing the gate from both directions. Once in a while she would test me by starting to pull toward the gate, but with a light tap of my foot she straightened back out and went where she was asked without offering to buck anymore.

"Stop her in the middle of the arena and let her know she did good," Ben said. "And Meghan, isn't everything easier now that she's listenin' to yer aids and bein' light for you? She wouldn't have got that way if you hadn't corrected her firmly when she needed it and then been nice to her when she did good."

He didn't wait for an answer, but loped his filly off into a circle. I think he just wanted me to think about it. And I had to admit he was right.

I stroked Savannah's neck and crooned to her. "What a smart girl you are to figure things out so fast. You're already starting to get soft and light. You're not just pretty, you're going to be a really nice horse!" And for the first time, I actually believed that.

Ben finally rode into the center with us and said, "Walk her forward a couple of steps to make sure she's awake and listenin'. Then stop her and ask for a turn on the forehand. Jes' turn her head a little to the left, drop yer left leg back a ways, and use it to push her hip around. If she tries to step forward, use yer other hand to kinda set the brake."

After a few steps at a walk, I stopped Savannah gently, then softly used my hands to turn her head. When I put my leg on her, she swung her hip away easily, while pivoting her body around her left front foot.

"Well, that was just about perfect!" Ben said. "Let her stand for a minute while I try it with this young'un."

Ben turned the filly's head and used his leg just the way I had, but the filly merely walked in a small circle. "This is where I set the brake with my outside hand, Meghan. Watch how I take hold just enough to stop her from movin' forward."

As Ben adjusted his hands, the filly took a single pivoting step around her left front leg. Ben immediately loosened the reins and said, "Whoa." He looked at me and said, "Yer turn. But try it off yer right rein and leg this time."

Chapter 11 - Dandelions

As softly and gently as I could, I asked Savannah to pivot over her right front foot. She went straight into a pretty turn on the forehand.

"Well, I'll be..." Ben chuckled. "I believe this little mare has more trainin' in her than we initially gave her credit for."

Ben then asked his filly for a turn on the forehand in the same direction he had gone the first time. This time she gave him one good step almost immediately. "She's a smart one," Ben said as he let her stop. "See how she's lickin' her lips and chewin'? That means she's thinkin' about what we did jes' now." He looked at Savannah. "You go on and put yer mare away. She's had a real good day and I don't wanna push her."

Back at the hitching rack, I unsaddled Savannah and walked her over to a patch of grass to let her graze, this time for twenty minutes.

While she munched on the grass, I started talking to her. "It won't be long before you can go out with the other horses, Savannah. You'll be even happier out there, I just know it. And you already seem to be a lot less... well, not to sound harsh or anything, but you seem less cranky than you used to be. You haven't tried to kick me for a few days now. Maybe we're starting to be friends."

I looked out at the pasture and felt a sudden twinge of sadness, remembering Rowdy. I tried to follow Ben's advice to think positively about how I was going to use what I learned from that grand old horse to help all the other horses I would ever ride, but that still didn't stop a fresh round of tears.

Watching Savannah through a blur of tears, I noticed that the mare almost seemed to go out of her way to grab a mouthful of dandelions.

"You like dandelions too! Rowdy loved them!" Somehow that made me feel a little better.

Violet's voice floated out from the barn door, "Meghan, come give me a hand with this."

Chapter 12
Violet

I hadn't realized that Violet was in the barn, so her sudden appearance surprised me. Quickly, I wiped the tears off my face with the back of my hand.

"Coming," I said, leading Savannah back to the barn and tying her up. Since Savannah's twenty minutes of grazing were over, I didn't really have an excuse not to go help.

As soon as I walked into the barn, Violet asked impatiently, "Can you open this can of hoof dressing? I'll break a fingernail if I keep trying. It's really stuck."

"Um, sure. I can try." I reached for the can and cranked on it as hard as I could. It didn't budge. Looking around for something that might help, I spotted Ben's fence tool on the bench in the tack room. "Your grandpa says he can use a fence tool for almost any project. Maybe it will work here." I tapped on the lid to loosen it, then wrapped the two sections of the handle around it to serve as a vise. With a quick twist, the lid came loose.

"Thanks," Violet said.

"You're welcome," I said, trying to remember if she had ever said anything nice to me up until this moment. Nothing came to mind. But then she said something that surprised me even more.

"Have you ever thought about running for princess for next year's rodeo?" she asked.

"Me? A rodeo princess?"

"Why not?" she asked. "You're a good rider. And you've got that long, wavy hair. With a little work, we could make it look really nice. I mean, you'd need to dress a lot better than you usually do, but I could help you pick out the right clothes and teach you how to use makeup. I think you could definitely win. Tryouts aren't until August, so there's time to get ready."

"Are you running again?" I asked.

"Not for princess," she laughed, though she sounded annoyed, not amused. "You have to be twelve years old or under to run for princess. You're twelve, aren't you?"

I nodded. "Yep! My birthday was just a couple of weeks ago."

"Well, then you're qualified. *I'm* going to run for Junior Rodeo Queen. I'm the Junior Queen Attendant this year."

"What do you do as the junior queen? Or the princess?" I asked.

"You'll see this weekend," she said. "You *are* coming to the rodeo, aren't you?"

"Oh, I hope so! My parents said we could probably go Thursday night!"

"See if you can get them to buy you some longer jeans before then."

I looked down self-consciously at my highwater pants. "I really have a hard time finding them long enough."

"Get your mom to take you to the farm supply store. One of my friends who's even taller than you works there, and she's able to get jeans that fit." Violet gave me one more disdainful glance before adding, "You need to start looking like a rodeo princess *now* if this is going to work."

⟨────

"Xender," I said, when he and I were filling water buckets later that day, "your sister was actually nice to me a while ago."

"She wants something," he said after thinking about it for approximately one nanosecond.

"Well, yeah, she wanted me to open the can of hoof dressing for her," I said.

He nodded knowingly. "Then as soon as you helped her, she went all cranky again, right?" It was a question, but he made it sound more like a statement of fact.

"Actually, no, she didn't."

"Was one of her boyfriends around at the time?" Xender asked. "Sometimes if someone she likes is watching, she even pretends to be nice to me."

"No. No boyfriend."

"Grandpa?"

"No, he wasn't around either."

"You're sure it was my sister?"

I giggled. "Yes, it was definitely Violet. I mean, she wasn't totally nice to me. She made fun of the way I dress and how my hair looks. But she also told me I was a good rider and that I should try out for rodeo princess."

"See? I told you she wanted something." Almost as an afterthought, he added, "You're not going to do it, are you?"

"I don't know," I answered. "I think it might be kind of fun."

"Oh no," Xender said, suddenly sounding like he had a stomach ache. "You are *not* going to start acting like Violet are you?"

"That depends. Does she like water fights?" I asked, aiming a bucket of water at him.

"No!" he yelled as he turned the hose toward me, managing to spray the back of my head as I spun away. "But I think I see what she means about how your hair looks," he laughed. "It looks kind of like a giant drowned rat."

The water fight went on long enough for both of us to look like drowned rats, *and* for Ol' Ben to tell us the horses didn't appear to be too bothered by us any more.

The Free Horse

Chapter 13
The Rodeo

The rodeo was really exciting! Mom and Dad bought tickets for the seats right in front of Ben and Xender, which was good because we could hear all of Ben's comments about the rodeo, but bad because it gave Xender too many chances to pester me. I was wearing my brand new, extra-long blue jeans and my nicest blouse, which made me feel pretty special. And Mom had styled my hair with her curling iron, so it actually looked nice. At least it did when we left our house. Between Xender tugging at it and the evening breeze, I wasn't sure how it looked by now.

There was so much to watch! Pretty soon, I forgot to think so much about myself and how I looked. Instead, I became engrossed in watching the rodeo. Xender must have too because he mostly quit tormenting me. The rodeo announcer called for the Grand Entry and the Rodeo Royalty came through the main gate one at a time. The girls carried various flags that flapped wildly as they galloped their horses in a giant circle around the arena. Violet smiled up at the people in the grandstand as her horse ran past us. The girls then stopped their horses in a line facing the crowd. The Rodeo Queen, who carried the American flag, rode forward a few steps so that she was in front of Violet and the other girls. Every girl except the Queen lowered her flag slightly in respect for our national flag.

The people in the grandstand all stood at the sight. The men took their hats off, and everyone put their hands over their hearts as the national anthem was sung. I noticed that, except for Violet, the girls were having trouble keeping their horses still. Several of the horses were pawing at the ground, while others were practically jumping up and down in place. Just after the last note of the song, the people in the grandstand let loose with a loud cheer, causing three of the horses to shy violently. One girl barely managed to stay on top her horse as he jumped sideways and then took off at a run. The rest of the Royalty galloped after her in a line, carrying their flags from the arena as the announcer began introducing the judges and officials.

"Violet's horse was certainly the best behaved, Ben," Mom observed.

"That's because Grandpa used to rope on him at the big rodeos and shows. That horse is used to everything!" Xender bragged.

The announcer's voice boomed over the loudspeakers: "Now if you'll give your attention to chute number one—" and all eyes turned to watch the first cowboy of the evening try to ride the first bucking horse.

"These are the bareback broncs," Xender said excitedly.

"Why is that rider leaning back so far?" Mom asked.

"Because when people fall off of horses, they usually fall off toward the front end," I told her.

"You would probably know that, as much experience as you've had lately," Dad said drily.

I felt my face turning red in embarrassment.

Ben came to my defense. "Meghan's not comin' off her mare too much any more. Between all the good trainin' that yer daughter has done on her and the work that chiropractor did, the little mare isn't inclined to buck so much these days. And she never did go at it as hard as these rodeo broncs," he said, just as a cowboy got bucked off in the arena.

I wanted to say that it sure felt as if she did, but I didn't want to contradict Ben. Or, more important, scare my parents.

"If a person's gonna ride, they're also gonna fall," Ben added. "It's part of the game. The trick is to learn how to prevent most of the situations where you *might* fall. And Meghan's learnin' more about that every day."

"I'm glad to hear *that*," Mom said.

One at a time, each bucking horse came out of the chute, determined to buck off an equally-determined cowboy who was trying his best to stay on board for the full eight seconds.

"I thought Jace Carlton was going to be in the bronc riding tonight," I said as the announcer proclaimed dramatically that the final bareback contestant for the evening had just earned the highest score.

Xender laughed at me. "He rides saddle broncs, not bareback broncs."

"When does that happen?" I asked.

"Not 'til after the steer wrestling and the team roping," Xender told me.

"They have steers that wrestle?" asked Dad.

I was pretty sure he was joking, but Ben answered him as if the question were serious. "In steer wrestlin' the cowboy has to catch up with a runnin' steer and then slide off his horse, grab the steer by the horns, and wrestle it to the ground. It's a timed event."

After the first steer wrestler finished, the Rodeo Queen rode into the arena and herded the steer across the arena, out the side gate, and back into the corrals where the rodeo livestock were kept.

"There's Violet!" said Mom, when Xender's sister rode in to herd the next steer out. We watched her as she expertly maneuvered the steer toward the gate, all the while maintaining a huge smile on her face. As soon as her job was done, she waved to the crowd and swept grandly out of the arena.

As the event continued, I found I was more interested in watching how the girls were handling their jobs than I was in watching the steer wrestling itself. I knew I would never be a steer wrestler, but if I got to be the Rodeo Princess next year, I might get to help herd cattle, like Violet was doing.

"This is my favorite event!" Xender shouted, as the team roping started.

Two riders backed their horses into the roping chutes at the end of the arena, one on either side of the cattle chute. Just after the steer was released from the chute, the riders galloped after him, swinging their lariats. One cowboy, the header, roped the steer's head and turned him to the side, while the second cowboy, the heeler, roped the animal's hind feet.

"I'm going to be a heeler!" Xender said excitedly. He was so intent on watching the team roping that he never poked me or tugged at my hair a single time during the entire event.

My luck held through the bareback bronc event too because Xender was so busy watching for Jace.

"No score!" said the announcer as the first contestant finished his ride.

"He stayed on the horse for the full eight seconds," Dad said. "Why didn't he get a score?"

"He didn't start him," Xender said, as if that clarified it.

The announcer explained it better. "The judges have ruled that the contestant's feet were not higher than the point of the horse's shoulders when he came out of the chutes, resulting in his disqualification. So put your hands together, folks, 'cause that's the only payback this cowboy's going to get this evening!"

The crowd obliged by clapping and cheering noisily.

I watched the next contestant carefully and saw that his feet and stirrups were way up on the horse's shoulders when the chute swung open. But even after the good start, the bucking horse managed to unload his rider in only two jumps.

"Looks like it's 'Horses – two, Cowboys – nothing'," declared the announcer.

"If this keeps up, Jace might actually stand a chance of earning some money tonight," said Xender.

But the next three contestants all had good rides, scoring well.

Xender started yelling, "There he is! There he is! There's Jace behind chute number two."

Chapter 14
Bucking and Barrels

I looked to see Jace climbing over the back of the chute, where he settled gingerly into his saddle, which was strapped on a very large horse with a thick black mane. The horse reared up, nearly smashing Jace in the narrow confines of the chute. Jace grabbed onto the far side wall and climbed up, away from the thrashing animal. When the bronc was standing quietly again, Jace eased down onto the saddle once more.

"How can his mother stand to watch him do this?" Mom asked, shielding her eyes with her hands, but then peeking out between her fingers to watch.

I wondered about Violet and glanced down toward the end of the arena, where I saw her standing up in her stirrups and looking over the fence as her hero prepared to make his ride.

I looked back just in time to see Jace nod his head. Suddenly the door of the chute opened and the bronc jumped out sideways, bucking. It looked to me like Jace had started him correctly, so that was good! Better still, he stayed on as the horse bucked for the next eight seconds, though it sure seemed more like eight minutes.

The crowd went wild, excited to see a hometown cowboy competing against professional rodeo riders. One of the pick-up men rode his horse next to the bronc and Jace jumped from his saddle, landing behind the pick-up man on the horse's rump. From there, he slid safely to the ground and doffed his hat to the crowd. The cheering from the grandstand got even louder. But when his score was announced, the enthusiastic cheering was replaced by only a smattering of applause along with some disappointed "Aahhhs."

"Why did he score so low?" asked Dad.

"Well," Ben said, "it probably wasn't him that scored low. It was probably the horse. See, the rider and the bronc each receive a score. The rider earns points for his ridin' style and the horse earns points for how hard he bucks. Jace probably scored okay for his part, but that horse wasn't much of a bucker. When they added the scores together for the total, he just couldn't catch the guys who rode the tougher broncs."

"He looked like he was bucking just fine to me," Mom said indignantly.

"Oh, he bucked okay, but he did it in a very rhythmic manner, goin' straight across the arena. He wasn't twistin' and turnin' or changin' up his timing the way the higher scorin' horses do. Jace just had bad luck in the draw."

"What's 'the draw'?" I asked.

"That's how they decide which cowboy gets to ride which horse," Xender said.

Another rider in the go-round outscored Jace, which dropped him into fifth place.

"That boy can be proud of himself," Ben said. "This is his first time competin' against the pros. Up 'til now he has just done high school and college rodeos."

The next event, tie-down roping, gave the royalty girls a chance to come back in the arena to herd each calf out after it was roped, or not roped, as the case might be.

The sun was slowly disappearing behind us over the western horizon, but the arena remained bright as day under the powerful lights that surrounded it.

"Don't the girls get to do anything at these rodeos other than carry flags and move cows?" asked Mom.

"There will be women competin' in the team ropin' this weekend," Ben said, "but apparently none of 'em drew up in tonight's go-round."

"But seriously," asked Dad, "would you want to watch *your* daughter in any of these events?"

"Well, no," Mom said. "But it just doesn't seem very equitable."

"The girls get their chance in the next event," Xender assured her.

"Barrel racing!" I said.

"The girls race barrels?" Dad asked. "You should try that event," he said, cuffing me on the shoulder. "I've seen you run and I am quite sure that you're faster than any barrel *I've* ever seen. Well, unless it's rolling downhill, but it's pretty flat out there in the arena. I would definitely bet on you."

"Thanks for your vote of confidence, Dad," I grinned, punching him back.

Some of the cowboys had set up three large barrels in a triangular pattern. The first contestant raced her horse into the arena. Passing the electric timer at the starting line she aimed for the first barrel over near the bucking chutes. She turned her horse in a tiny right-hand circle around the barrel and sped toward the second one, which was right in front of the grandstand. After making a left-hand turn around it, she ran her horse toward the third barrel in the middle of the arena toward the far end. Circling it to the left, she then galloped back across the finish line.

After each contestant's run, the announcer told us the time she had earned. Most of the times were in the 17-second range, but several riders were in the 16's.

It was interesting watching the different techniques the girls—actually women, mostly—were using to get the most speed and best turns out of their horses. I noticed that the ones who turned the quickest and closest around the barrels were getting the fastest times. I wanted to talk to Ben about it, but the crowd was too noisy for me to hear him unless I turned around. And I didn't want to miss a second.

Chapter 14 - Bucking and Barrels

If a horse knocked down a barrel, the crowd would let out an "Oohhh" of sympathy, and the rider would have a five-second penalty added to her time.

By the time the barrel racing was over, the sky was completely dark.

"The crowd is really getting noisy," Mom shouted.

Ben shouted back, "They're gettin' revved up for the bull riding. That's generally the favorite event."

"That's why it's the final contest of the night," Xender shouted. "It's the most dangerous too!"

The Free Horse

Chapter 15
Send in the Clowns

"Why is bull riding considered more dangerous than the bronc riding?" Mom asked loudly, struggling to make her question heard over the noise of the rodeo fans.

"Because horses won't usually try to kill a fella after they buck him off. But bulls will," shouted Ben. "You'll notice that most of these bull riders are wearin' helmets and safety vests to help protect 'em in case somethin' goes amiss."

"And those guys dressed up like clowns aren't just clowns. They're bullfighters. They help keep the bulls from stomping on the cowboys after they've hit the ground," Xender shouted. "They're super cool!"

They were seriously brave too. It was amazing to watch them run between a charging bull and a cowboy who was down in the dirt. They would distract the bull, giving the cowboy time to get up and run—or limp—to safety. One time a cowboy got his hand stuck in the rope that was tied around the bull's body. When he got bucked off, his hand wouldn't come loose. The bull continued to buck and spin while the cowboy was dragged along by his arm and shaken like a rag doll. Immediately, one of the bullfighters ran right up to the bull and tried to get the cowboy's hand free. A second bullfighter kept trying to distract the bull so he'd quit spinning. It looked as if the bull was stepping on the cowboy every time he came down on the ground.

Finally, the cowboy's hand came loose and he dropped into the dirt, where he lay completely still. The bullfighter who had freed the man's hand stepped between him and the bull and got the bull to chase him. The second bullfighter then stepped in and got the bull's attention so that the huge animal turned and chased him instead. The two traded off like that until they had put some distance between the bull and the injured cowboy. Then two other men on horses took over and managed to herd the bull toward the stock gate and out of the arena. The bull stopped at the gate, his head high in the air. He snorted, as if to say, "I won," before trotting down the lane beyond the gate.

I took a breath, realizing I had been holding it for the last minute or so, a minute that felt more like an hour. It was oddly quiet in the grandstand. I think everyone else must have been holding their breath too. All eyes focused on the man lying in the dirt. The bullfighters and several other cowboys ran over to him. Medics from the ambulance that sat just outside the gate raced in, carrying their medical bags. Before they could reach him though, the cowboy slowly started to stand up. To my amazement, he limped out of the arena without even leaning on the arm of any of the men who surrounded him.

The crowd went crazy, clapping and cheering.

Incredibly, the rodeo went on as if nothing unusual had happened. Several riders got bucked off before the eight-second buzzer was heard. One of them got butted by the bull as he ran for safety. The bull tossed him up in the air and probably would have attacked him again if one of the bullfighters hadn't gotten between them. But four of the riders rode the full eight seconds and earned scores for their rides. The crowd cheered their approval every time that happened.

After the final bull rider received his score, the announcer's voice boomed, "For another exciting per-formance of America's greatest home-grown sport, come back tomorrow evening at seven! And don't miss the rodeo parade at five on Saturday, right down the middle of town, followed by the championship finals at seven!"

We stood up, stretched, and followed the crowd out of the grandstand. Ben and Xender went to find Violet, so they could load her horse into the trailer and drive home. Mom, Dad and I turned toward the parking lot.

"Can we go on one of the rides before we go home?" I asked, looking at the lights from the carnival that was set up beyond the grandstand.

Mom answered, "Sorry, sweetie, but your dad has to work tomorrow, and it will be past ten before we get home, even if we leave right now."

"Aww, honey, I think I can stay up a little longer if our favorite daughter wants to go on one of the rides." Turning toward me, he asked, "Which one looks like the most fun to you?"

"Let's go take a closer look!" I said, turning toward the carnival!

Chapter 16
This Cowgirl Won't Quit

"It seems as if the rodeo horses must have a pretty hard life," I said while cleaning the stalls the next morning.

"Are you kidding?" asked Xender. "They work for eight lousy seconds, once or twice a week."

"But what about those straps they had around their flanks to make them buck?" I asked.

"Those don't hurt. They just kind of annoy them and encourage them to buck," he said. "Those horses and bulls *like* to buck."

"How do you know that?" I demanded.

"Because if they didn't, the stock contractors wouldn't have bought them in the first place. Before you moved here, one of the ranchers Grandpa's done work for had a horse that kept bucking his hired hands off. He was going to send him to Grandpa to see if he could train him not to, but then the owner heard that a stock contractor was going to be at the fairgrounds trying out potential rough stock. They took the horse in and he bucked so well that the contractor bought him for a lot more than he was worth as a ranch horse."

"Do you know if the horse is still working as a bucking horse?" I asked.

"Yep. In fact he's here this weekend. He didn't buck last night, but Grandpa and I walked back through the stock pens before the rodeo started and saw him. He looked good. All those horses did. They're worth too much to the stock contractor not to take care of them."

"Well, I guess that's not so bad then," I said.

"Think about it, Meghan. We've been working a whole lot longer this morning than any of those horses are going to have to work all summer, so don't be feeling too sorry for them."

Once we were done cleaning stalls, we brushed and saddled our horses. I took Savannah to the round pen, while Xender went to the arena where his grandpa was working a training horse.

In less than ten minutes, I heard Ol' Ben holler, "Savannah's lookin' good. Get her over here and hop up on her."

As I put the bridle on, I actually smiled. "Good girl, Savannah. You didn't even care when I put it over your ears."

"Let's see what she remembers from yesterday," Ben said.

I mounted up and began working her around the arena. The first time we passed the gate, she made a half-hearted attempt to pull toward it, but with just a light touch of my legs, I kept her on track. We did circles and serpentines all over the arena at both a walk and a trot.

"Yer hands are gettin' a lot softer, Meghan!" said Ben.

My insides felt all happy and I couldn't stop the smile on my face.

"I think it's time to ask her for a lope," Ben continued.

My smile faded. The good feeling I'd had was instantly replaced by a nasty churning in my stomach. Except for when she had shied from things, most of the times Savannah had bucked me off had been when we had tried to canter. Adding to my worries, Savannah was suddenly trotting faster and sticking her head up in the air.

"Bend her around, Meghan," Ben yelled, "don't let her act like that." After a pause, he asked, "What happened back there? Why do you think she suddenly got all excited and racy?"

I wanted to say I didn't know, but deep down, I did. "I guess I got nervous."

"I thought that might've been it," Ben said. "You don't need to get all worried over this, Meghan. She's not goin' to do anything you can't handle."

When I had her jogging nicely again, Ben said, "Go ahead and lope her when you get to that next corner. Jes' sit back a little, in case she wants to crow hop. If she does, you be ready to take her head to the inside and kick her."

I took a deep breath, leaned back a little, and signaled her for a canter. She just trotted faster. I kicked her harder and she shook her head in annoyance, but still wouldn't lope.

"You've *asked* her and you've *told* her," Ben yelled. "Now you *make* her do it! Swat her on her butt with the end of yer reins whilst you kick her."

I did as he said and she jumped into a canter, crow hopping on her first stride.

"Bend her around so she can't keep tryin' to buck, and then you kick her hard enough that she takes notice of you," Ben commanded. "Swat her on the butt a couple of times while you're bendin' her. She needs to learn that there are repercussions to her bad behavior."

Once more, I was almost dizzy before we stopped.

"Now take her back out toward the corner and ask her—real nice—to lope again."

I was scared, but Ben had taught me that cowgirls don't quit, so I put the fear out of my head and did what I needed to. This time she stepped into a canter when I asked.

I was surprised—no, actually, I was thrilled—to realize that her lope wasn't all rough and disjointed

94

like it used to be! It just felt like a nice, normal canter! But after only about four strides, she broke back into a trot.

"Keep her goin', Meghan! You should've felt that comin' and done somethin' about it before she quit ya," Ben said.

I asked her to canter again, and she went into it pretty easily. A minute or two later, when I felt her try to slow down, I sat back and squeezed with my legs. She continued to canter, a little too fast, but not unpleasantly.

"Well, look at that. She's almost like a real horse," Xender said, which was as close to a compliment as he had given her so far.

"Bend her inside, drop her down to a trot, and then lope her out the other way," Ben said.

She came back to a trot easily when I turned her, but then she didn't want to step back into a canter in the new direction when I asked. I kicked harder. Still nothing. I sat back, kicked harder and swatted her on the butt.

"Good girl!" Ben yelled as the mare cantered.

She hadn't crow hopped either!

By the time we were done working her, I was breathing hard, as if I'd just run my fastest mile ever.

"I sure hope no one ever again tries to tell me riding isn't a sport because the horse is doing all the work, or I'm... I'm..." I was panting too hard to finish.

Xender laughed. "I got in trouble in fifth grade once, 'cause I got in a fight with one of the basketball players who said that to me."

He turned away to work his horse and Ben rode over to me. "You did a fine job, Meghan. You were fair but firm and that's what it takes to be a good trainer. I'm mighty proud of you."

I smiled again, the happy feelings I'd had earlier flooding back inside of me.

"This little mare has got into some bad habits over time; probably from the pain she was sufferin' in her neck and back and also 'cause she's a little bit spoiled," Ben said. "But I don't think she's a bad horse. In fact, the more I see, the more I think she might once have had some decent trainin'. Did you notice she never once took a wrong lead with you today?"

I nodded. I had seen Ben retrain several horses that wanted to "lead" with the left front leg when they were cantering to the right, or vice versa. It had made the horses seem awkward and unbalanced. I was glad Savannah didn't have that bad habit. She had enough of them without adding that to the mix.

"You're goin' to have to continue to be cautious when you ask her to lope, because that habit of wantin' to crow hop and buck is goin' to take consistency on yer part if you want to make her quit it. But I do believe that if you don't go fallin' off of her anymore, you can get it done," he said, smiling. "And now that you know how to correct her faster, I don't guess you'll be lettin' her stuff yer head in the dirt quite so often."

"I like it up here a whole lot better," I said.

"Yeah, well that's the basic definition of ridin', isn't it?" Ben said. "Keep yer horse between you and the ground."

"Sounds good to me!" I giggled.

While we were unsaddling the horses, Ben said, "I think it's time you turned yer mare out in the pasture, Meghan."

"Really?" I asked, excited for her and happy for me because I wouldn't have to clean out the round pen every day.

"Let's give it a try," he said, walking toward the pasture. I followed, leading Savannah.

The Free Horse

Chapter 17
The Pecking Order

Xender was already at the pasture gate, where he had just turned Scout loose. When he saw me leading Savannah toward him, he said, "This ought to be interesting."

Before I could ask what he meant, Ben said, "Lead her into the pasture and then turn her around so she's facin' the gate before you unbuckle her halter. Soon as you've got it off of her head, step back toward the gate. That way, if she wheels around and kicks out, she won't hit ya."

I did as Ben said and just as he predicted, Savannah wheeled around and bucked, kicking her hind feet high in the air.

"She's not tryin' to kick you, Meghan. She's just feelin' some joy," Ben said. "But you always want to be prepared for that 'cause gettin' kicked 'cause of joy hurts just as much as gettin' kicked 'cause of meanness.

Savannah bucked and kicked a few more times and then took off at a run across the pasture to get to the small herd of horses.

They watched her coming with interest. Ben's cutting horse came out of the small herd to greet her, but after barely sniffing noses, he flattened his ears, turned, and kicked her. Immediately he spun back around and bit her on her neck. Savannah fled from him, but he chased her, biting her at every opportunity. His attack went on for what seemed like forever, but probably wasn't more than thirty seconds. Then Scout approached her, ears flattened, and bit her too. She ran off from him and met up with a mare. The two sniffed noses, squealed and struck out at each other with their front feet before the mare turned and kicked at Savannah. After a few more run-ins, Savannah ran from the herd far enough that no one else could kick her or bite her. Finally, everyone settled down and resumed grazing.

"Your eyes are about as big as baseballs," Xender laughed. "What'd you think was going to happen?"

"I don't know. But n— n— not that," I stuttered.

Ben said, "They jes' had to let her know who's in charge. Have you ever heard the term 'peckin' order,' Meghan?"

"Well, yeah. I guess. But I thought that had to do with chickens."

"It does," Ben agreed. "But it applies to horses too. In every herd of horses, no matter how big or how small, there's one boss horse. Then there's a number two horse who can boss around everyone except the boss. Then there's a number three horse, and on down the line 'til you get to the horse at the bottom of the peckin' order. That one don't get to boss anyone around. He—or she—just has to stay out of everyone else's way and be glad to have a herd to be part of. And they *are* glad. Horses like to have a leader. That's how nature made 'em. They feel safer with a strong leader."

"Is Savannah going to be okay after all the kicking and biting?" I asked.

"Oh, she'll have a few cuts and bruises on her, but nothin' life-threatenin'," Ben said.

"I don't see any blood," Xender observed.

"If you think about it, Meghan, this is what I was telling you the day Savannah was magnetized to the gate and wanted to stop and go to it every time you trotted past. Remember? It's how horses communicate. They suggest to her with their ears that she should move outta their way. That's the 'ask'. If she doesn't get the hint, they threaten to kick her. That's the 'tell'. If she's still standin' where they don't want her, they explain she has made a big mistake by followin' through with a kick or a bite. That's the 'make'," Ben explained.

"They're sure a lot tougher on each other than we are on them," I said.

Ben chuckled. "Well, our way of trainin' *is* based on how horses already communicate. We're just not as ornery about it as they are."

Ben and Xender finally walked back to the barn, but I sat down in the grass and watched the horses. Once in a while, Savannah would graze her way closer to one of the others. Each time, that horse would flatten his ears at her and swing his head in her direction. She would immediately put a little more distance between them. She was definitely learning her place in the pecking order, and that place appeared to be at the very bottom.

"I was thinking about it," I told Xender the next day, "and it kind of reminded me of school."

"What do you mean?" Xender asked.

"Watching Savannah figure out her place. I mean, it seems to me there's a pecking order at school too."

Xender laughed. "Yeah. I guess there is. I hadn't thought about it like that."

"Remember when we started sixth grade last year?" I asked him.

"Yeah, I sure do! A couple of the eighth graders saw me in the boys room and said they were gonna give me a swirly," Xender said.

"I didn't know that!"

"Yeah, well it's not exactly something I wanted to brag about," he said.

"How'd you get out of it?" I hesitated. "Or did you?"

102

Chapter 17 - The Pecking Order

"I told them they should wait a few weeks 'til my hair grew longer, 'cause a buzz cut like mine wasn't going to be worth the effort. That made them laugh."

"And they let you go?"

"I'm not sure if they would have or not, but I also asked one of them how his dad was liking the rope horse that Grandpa trained for him. When he realized I knew his dad, I guess he started thinking that dunking my head in the toilet might not be a wise plan."

"Wow! I'm glad I never had to go through anything like that. I'd have been scared," I admitted. "The worst I got was shoved a few times when I was walking down the hallway. And called a few nasty names."

"What'd you do?"

"I ignored the name callers, and eventually they stopped.

"What about the shovers?" Xender asked.

"That was mostly just one girl. So one time, when I saw her coming down the hall, I waited 'til she shoved me, then one of my elbows kinda connected really hard with her head. Then right away I started apologizing that somehow I had tripped and had hit her accidentally. She *knew* it wasn't an accident, and she figured out I wasn't going to take it any more without fighting back, so she quit trying to bully me."

"What would you have done if she *had* fought back?" Xender asked.

"Fallen down, I suspect."

He laughed.

"No, seriously, this girl's not as tall as me, but she packs a lot more weight. I'm pretty sure she would've flattened me. But there were teachers in the hallway, so I didn't think she would try it."

"You were lucky. She could've decked you sometime when there weren't any teachers around."

"Yeah, I suppose she could've. But she didn't. And she didn't bother me anymore either."

"Well, it's going to take more than one time to convince Savannah that she shouldn't mess with you. She's been a spoiled brat for a long time," Xender said.

"What makes you say that?"

"People don't usually give away a nice-looking, sound horse for no reason," he replied.

"Cool! You just admitted she's nice-looking!" I exulted.

"Oh, that's not the point!" he said, shaking his head. "She is kind of okay looking, but who cares what she looks like if she's a witch to deal with?"

A few days later, I almost got dumped again.

Chapter 18
Who's the Leader?

I was having a great morning riding Savannah. I was thrilled at how much she was improving every day, getting softer and lighter to my cues. Ben told me to stay in the arena and work her on turns on the forehand while he and Xender went back to the barn to get fresh horses. She finished a really nice turn to the right, but when I stopped her and started to pet her on the neck, her head shot up in the air and she looked around, wild-eyed. Suddenly, she bolted toward the gate.

I was barely able to pull her head around to my knee, which kept her from running away with me. I continued turning her and trying to get her attention back on me, but she was frantic, whinnying and screaming for the other horses. Even with her nose almost at my knee, she kept trying to jump out from under me toward the gate. But at least she couldn't actually buck. She just kept bouncing up and down, turning and running sideways, trying to unload me. I leaned back to keep her from pulling me off.

Forcing myself to sound calm, I started talking to her in my most soothing voice. "Why do you want to go with them, you silly girl? They don't even like you. They're always mean to you out in the pasture. I know you want a leader to take care of you, but honest, Savannah, if you'll trust me, I can be your leader. You need to start trusting me, girl." I continued talking to her as calmly as I could, bending her and leaning back the whole time.

Finally, she stopped screaming and began responding to my aids. She wasn't exactly light about it, and I was afraid Ben would be mad at me for pulling on her so much. Eventually she began to relax and listen to me and I was able to ease up a little bit. I put her into a trot and began making circles and serpentines all over the arena, bending her left, then right, then left again, and always talking to her. Finally I got her to the farthest end of the arena, away from the gate, and trotted her through a whole series of small figure eights, keeping her busy so she wouldn't freak out again.

I was focusing so hard on the mare that it startled me when I heard Ben's voice close by. "Well, you handled that like a real trainer," he said quietly.

I looked up to see him leaning on the fence, watching.

When I broke my concentration by looking up at Ben, Savannah tried to bolt with me again. But I quickly got her back on the figure-eight and listening to me.

"Well done," Ben said. "You just keep workin' her like you're doin'. I told Xender to go fill water buckets and keep himself busy around the barn until you get done with this trainin' session. I don't want any other horses out here until you win this round, which, it seems to me, you're doin'."

Savannah was finally getting more relaxed and more attentive so I stepped her out into a canter. Her head went up a little as she tried to look toward the barn, but I bent her around, trotted her a few steps and then went off in the other direction at a canter again.

Finally, Ben said, "When you decide she's listenin' to ya, stop her and let her stand. But make sure you stop her headin' away from the barn."

The next time around, I stopped her. She stood for only a few seconds before she started to fidget and whinney.

"Lope her off again, Meghan!" Ben commanded.

I put her back to work. She quieted down again pretty quickly, so I stopped her again. This time she stood still.

"You know you're not done yet, don't you?" Ben asked.

I wasn't sure what he meant and he didn't wait for me to ask.

"You're gonna have to get her back to the barn without her goin' all stupid on you again. As soon as you climb down off her back and start to turn her toward the barn, she's likely gonna get in a big hurry, forgettin' who her leader is. So you're goin' to have to keep remindin' her, which you can do by turnin' her or stoppin' and backin' her up every single time her mind wanders," he explained. "Now, you go on and climb down, but you make real sure that you keep her attention. When you're workin' with her, there has got to be no one in her world except *you*. And if she forgets that, you need to remind her, firmly but fairly. *You* are the benevolent despot!"

"The what?" I asked.

"Do you know what 'benevolent' means?" Ben asked.

"Uh, not really," I admitted.

"Well, it means kind. It means someone who does stuff out of the goodness of his heart. Or in your case, her heart." He continued, "Then there's despot. Do you know that one?"

I shook my head.

"Well, that means the ruler. The king. It's the person whose word is law." Ben laughed. "Kinda like me. Around here, I'm the despot. What I say, goes."

I heard a different voice laugh. "Oh Grandpa, you're so funny."

It was Violet. I don't think I had ever heard Violet laugh before. Or at least not a real laugh that sounded as if she was actually happy and not just trying to impress a boy or to make fun of her brother. I was so surprised that I forgot for a split second that I was holding Savannah, but that was enough for the mare to try to take advantage of the situation. She bolted for the barn, nearly jerking the reins out of my hands. Somehow I managed to hold on and get her turned. I quickly began making Savannah trot a small circle around me. After a few times around, I stopped her and backed her up.

"That was quick thinkin'," Ben said. "Now that you've got her mind back on you, keep it there all the way to the barn."

It took a lot of effort, but I managed to keep her listening to me and I finally got her back to the hitching rack. Just as I did, Ben and Xender were untying their horses and going to the arena.

"We're leavin' you on purpose," Ben said. "That mare has got to learn to depend on you as her leader; not the horses around her. Keep her brain occupied while you get her unsaddled and back out to the pasture. While you're out there, catch Freckles, bring him in, and saddle him up. You're goin' to ride him today too."

Later, as I led Savannah to the pasture, I saw Violet coming the other way, leading her paint horse toward the gate. We got there about the same time and she actually opened the gate for me.

"Thanks," I said as I led Savannah through.

"I'm sorry if I distracted you or your horse out in the arena," she said, sounding as if she meant it.

I was so surprised I had trouble getting my tongue untangled. "No, that was— You didn't— You were fine," I said, hoping I didn't sound as much like a total moron as I was pretty sure I did.

She didn't say anything more about it. Instead she asked, "When do you want to get together to learn how to do makeup and fix your hair for the contest?"

"Oh, um, I'm not sure. Uh, the contest isn't until the beginning of August, right?" I asked.

A hint of her usual annoyance came back into her voice, "You can't wait 'til then, Meghan. You're going to have to practice so you can get your technique down."

"Well, when's a good time for you?" I asked.

She brightened. "How about tomorrow afternoon, after you're all done riding and doing chores? You can go home, wash your hair and come back over to the house and then we'll have your first lesson on hair and makeup!"

"Okay. Sure. If that works for you," I told her, attempting to sound excited, rather than slightly nervous like I was really feeling. Well, actually, seriously nervous.

Chapter 19
Feelings

After turning Savannah loose, I started toward Freckles. He saw me coming, but instead of meeting me as he usually did, he walked away a few steps. I was surprised and a little hurt that he would do that. I followed after him and caught him.

Back at the hitching rack, Ben asked casually, "What was bothering you when you went out to catch Freckles?"

"Uh... nothing."

"Something must've been. I've never seen him walk away like that before," Ben said. "Were you upset about something?"

"No, not really. Why? What's that got to do with it?" I asked.

"Everything," Ben said. "Horses know how we're feeling. If we're angry or upset, they'd just as soon stay away from us. You can't fool a horse."

"Hmm. Maybe I was feeling a little nervous," I admitted.

"Nervous about ridin' Freckles?" he asked in surprise, "'cause if he scares you, you don't need to be gettin' on him."

"Oh, no!" I protested. "I love riding Freckles! He's the best! I was worrying about something else. If I'd been thinking about riding Freckles, I'd have been nothing but happy!"

Ben looked at me for a long moment. "Well, as long as you're sure, go ahead and saddle up."

I turned my focus away from Violet and thought about Freckles instead, which made me feel a whole lot calmer. While I brushed and saddled him, Ben said, "I don't know how they do it, but horses can sense fear, anger, or nervousness in other horses and also in the people around them. That's how Mother Nature made 'em. In the wild, they live in herds for safety. If one horse in the herd sees a mountain lion, the other horses can all sense the first one's fear, and they go on high alert."

"But how can they sense what people are feeling?" I asked.

"I don't rightly know. I just know that they do. I've even read scientific experiments about it. Someone put a heart monitor on a horse and a second monitor on the handler. They told the handler to lead the horse around an arena three times, past a guy with an umbrella. They told him that the first two times they walked past him, the man wouldn't do anything.

But the third time, they told the handler, the man was goin' to pop the umbrella open. When the handler started gettin' close to the guy with the umbrella the third time, her heart rate shot up 'cause she knew she was about to get drug around the arena by a terrified horse. Soon as her heart rate went up, the horse's did too."

"I'd sure be scared if I knew someone was going to pop an umbrella open in front of my horse's face," I agreed.

"Yeah, well that's the kicker," Ben said. "The guy with the umbrella never actually opened it. So the horse never had a reason to react to the umbrella. All he felt was the handler's fear. But that was enough for him."

"Wow! That's amazing."

With even more determination, I kept thoughts of Violet, Savannah, and anything else that might worry me out of my head and concentrated on how much fun Freckles was and how much I was learning on him. And I had a great ride! Afterward, while I was cooling him out, I asked Ben about Savannah's behavior this morning.

"Do you think I got scared and that's what upset Savannah?"

"Nope. I don't believe that was it. I think she just got upset 'cause the other horses left her. Horses are gregarious creatures, Meghan."

"What's that mean?" Today was turning into a veritable vocabulary lesson.

"It's like I was sayin' earlier, they want to be with their friends, be part of a herd. That's how nature made 'em. They feel safer that way."

"I guess I'm not very gregarious then," I told him. "I don't like crowds. I'd rather be with a horse any day."

Chapter 20
Transformation

"You're kidding, right?" Violet was looking at me with a combination of disbelief and disgust. "You've never experimented with using makeup? Not even once?"

I shook my head.

"Why not?" she demanded.

"I don't know," I mumbled. "I guess I just never thought much about it. I mean, horses don't care what I look like, so I never cared either." Even I cringed a bit when I said that, feeling quite certain that if there was a contest for lame remarks, I would easily win with that one.

Violet was shaking her head. Then she started laughing. "You *are* about the most horse-crazy person I know. Worse than Xender even, and that's going some. Grandpa was so happy when you started riding horses here. It really made me mad."

115

I must have looked as startled as I felt.

"Oh, it's okay. I don't hate you anymore," she said. "I did at first though. But then I realized that with you to clean stalls and help with chores, I was off the hook and had more time to do the stuff I wanted to do. Grandpa doesn't push me to ride as much anymore, now that you're around. It's really nice."

"But you're such a good rider," I said.

"Oh, please. I've got about as much interest in riding horses as you've got in makeup. I ride because I have to. I only *look* as if I know what I'm doing because I ride horses Grandpa trained. I am not even slightly interested in learning the family business." She paused before continuing, "Now *you* are going to work at learning proper techniques for putting on makeup, even though *you* clearly aren't interested in it, just like *I* had to learn to ride."

"What got you so interested in this stuff?" I asked.

"When I was little, I went over to the neighbor's one morning and knocked on the door. A woman opened it, and I asked her if Pam was there. She started laughing and said that she was Pam. I didn't believe her, 'cause Pam was a really beautiful woman, but the gal at the door was just this side of ugly."

"So… was it?" I asked.

"Was it what?" Violet responded.

"Was it Pam at the door?"

"Yeah, it was," Violet laughed. "But without her makeup on and her hair done, she didn't look anything like the Pam I was used to seeing. That's when I realized how much difference a person could make in themselves with a little bit of make-up. That was also the day I knew what my career was going to be!"

"What's that?" I asked.

Violet flashed a smile that lit up the whole room, then she whispered, "I'm going to go to cosmetology school. In fact, I'm going to start classes at the community college while I'm still in high school. I've already talked to the high school counselor about it!"

"Wow!" I didn't know what else to say, but I guess that must have been enough because she talked a mile a minute for the next hour about color palettes for both the clothing I should be wearing and the makeup I should use, and how to apply that makeup, and how I should style my hair.

The whole time she talked, she worked on my face and my hair, showing me what to do. I watched in the mirror while she transformed me from "me" into someone who looked—I don't know—different. It seemed really weird to see my mirror image speaking when I spoke, blinking when I blinked, and reacting when I did, but the image wasn't the "me" I was used to seeing.

"Kinda freaky, huh?" she said.

"I look freaky?" I asked, surprised.

"No, you dork! I mean it's kinda freaky seeing the changes in your own face with a good makeup job," she said. "Look at you. You're really pretty."

Okay, that *was* seriously freaky. Having Violet say something as nice as that.

"Now listen. I've written down a list of the cosmetics we used, including the brand names and specific colors. Get your mom to buy these for you before we get together again, so you can practice putting on your *own* makeup," she said.

"Um, okay."

Violet looked at me sharply. "You're going to have to put some time into learning this. It takes practice, just like riding a horse takes practice."

"I'll practice. I promise." What else could I say?

I managed to slip past the barn without being seen by either Xender or Ben, which made me happy. I wasn't sure how I was feeling about this new look, and I definitely did not want to hear their opinions until I could figure out my own.

As I walked out the lane toward home, my ninja luck ran out. Both of my parents were sitting on the back deck and saw me at the same time. Dad was the first to react.

"Wow!" he said, followed by a slow whistle.

"Oh, sweetie, you look gorgeous," Mom gushed.

"Do you really like it?" I asked, feeling myself blush as my parents stared at me.

"How could we not?" Dad said. "Our beautiful little girl has been transformed into a beautiful young lady!"

"You look so grown up! Whoever did your makeup did a fantastic job of highlighting your looks instead of disguising them, the way some girls do," Mom said. "Who did you tell me was going to help you? Was it Violet?"

I nodded.

"Well I never expected anything this professional."

That reminded me of the list Violet had given me. I pulled it out of my pocket and gave it to Mom.

Every day, from then on, I practiced with my new makeup in the late afternoons, after I got home from the barn, but before my parents showed up. I don't think Violet believed I was working at it because I wouldn't let anyone see me. And Xender was kind of annoyed with me for leaving early almost every day and refusing to say why. But I worked at it faithfully and finally started to get faster with the process and more comfortable with the result. It was actually kind of fun knowing I could do this. I mean, the horses still weren't going to care what I looked like. But when school started in August, I was going to be able to look really nice. If I wanted to.

The Free Horse

Chapter 21
Found Out

"There's a little schoolin' show over in Durango this next weekend," Ben said one morning as we headed out to the arena. "It'd be a fine opportunity for you to see how yer little mare is goin' to respond to a new place and to the pressures of the show ring. There are even some pattern classes, like Horsemanship, so you can practice for the pattern you'll have to ride for yer Royalty contest."

"That sounds like fun!" I said, mostly meaning it. But immediately, I started to worry. "Do you think we're ready for something like that?"

"Well if you're not," Ben chuckled, "it'd be best to find out now, so we know what to work on while we've still got a little time to fix it, don't ya think?"

All week, Ben worked us on some of the things we needed to know before going into a show ring. "Here's what the judge will be lookin' for," he would say before explaining the intricacies of a Western Pleasure class and how it differed from a Horsemanship class.

"But here's what's even more important," Ben said. "You need to remember that you have no control over the judge. The only thing *you* can control is how you are ridin'. And truth to tell, that is the only thing that matters. In every single event you need to go out there and give your horse the best ride you can—the ride yer horse needs. If you do that, you'll come out of the show pen happy. If the judge thinks you and yer horse were a good team, he—or she—might give you a ribbon fer yer efforts. But those ribbons? They're jes' the icin' on the cake. Helpin' yer horse gain confidence is the main thing."

Meanwhile, Violet coached me on my selection of clothes for the show. "You've got to look the part," she told me. "You want that judge to take you seriously the minute you ride through the gate. So you're going to wear the right clothes and you're going to wear makeup."

"In front of other people?" I blurted out.

"Yes!" she practically shouted. "You need to start getting used to it."

I ground the toe of my boot into the dirt and looked at my hands, my horse—anything but Violet's eyes.

"Are you sure I look okay wearing it?"

"No, I'm not," she retorted.

I looked at her. That wasn't exactly the answer I had expected.

"Well how would I know how you look with it? You tell me you're practicing the techniques I taught you, but you never show your face when you're wearing it. So, no. I don't know."

I looked back down at my hands.

"But I'm going to know tomorrow, because you are going to show up for chores in the morning made up as if it's the day of the show! And you're going to leave your makeup on all day. You're not even going to risk ruining it by having one of those stupid water fights with my obnoxious little brother. Got it?"

I gave her the answer that the tone of her voice demanded.

"Yes."

"What's the matter with you?" Xender asked as we finished mucking out the pens the next morning.

"Nothing? Why?" I asked, continuing to focus my attention downward, toward the few remaining road apples.

"Beause the last time I saw someone who wouldn't look up was last spring, when Matt Scanlon showed up at school with a black eye after his baby sister punched him."

The road apples became increasingly fascinating to me.

"Meghan!" he fairly shouted. "Look at me!"

123

I looked at him and didn't even slightly like the way his face suddenly twisted.

"Ohhhh, gross," he said in disgust. "You look like my sister."

He grabbed the handles of the wheelbarrow, shoved it out through the gate and stomped off toward the manure pile to dump it.

I rescued the apple picker he'd left behind, locked the gate to the pen, and headed for the barn to put the equipment away. Since I was fairly sure I didn't really look like his pretty sister, I wondered what he really meant by that. Lost in thought, I nearly ran into Ben, who stopped and did a double take.

"Well, look at you," he said slowly. "You look plumb purty."

"Thanks," I mumbled.

"You know what?" he asked, sounding as if an important thought had just hit him. "You should try lookin' like that tomorrow. That'd be real nice in the show pen." He nodded. "Yep. Mighty nice."

Okay. The current score was one against and one for. I wondered what the tiebreaker would say when she showed up.

I didn't have long to wait. Violet arrived at the barn a few minutes later, walked straight up to me and silently scrutinized my makeup job. Slowly, a smile began to spread across her face.

"I didn't think you'd really been working on it," she said bluntly. "But you have! And you look good!"

"Your brother hates it."

"My brother is clueless."

"Ben said I should look like this for the horse show."

"Absolutely!" she agreed. "That's a pretty little mare you've got, and you've done a good job training her. Now you need to show her to her best advantage. And that includes not detracting from her because *you* don't look your best."

We gave the horses we were taking to the show an easy workout and then bathed them and cleaned tack. Despite all the water around, I didn't have to worry about getting into a water fight with Xender. He hadn't talked to me or even gotten within fifty feet of me since he had stormed away this morning.

The Free Horse

Chapter 22
Ring Sour

Unloading Savannah out of the horse trailer at the fairgrounds in Durango, I looked around to see how many of the other contestants had decided to show up as early as we had. I only saw one other trailer. I was okay with that since I felt like a total dork at the moment, wearing an apron to keep my shirt and pants clean while I got Savannah ready. But Violet had insisted.

Violet and I tied our horses on the side of the trailer near the tack room door. Xender mumbled something unintelligible and walked Scout to the opposite side to tie him up.

"Get yer horses brushed and saddled," Ben said, "while I go say howdy to Lane Nelson. At least, I think that's Lane over there. Haven't seen him in a month of Sundays."

"Which bridles do you want us to use, Grandpa?" Violet asked.

"Use the ones you plan to compete in. As shiny as you've got those horses lookin', you wouldn't want to let 'em be seen in their plain ol' ranch bridles, would ya?" He winked, turned, and walked toward Mr. Nelson's trailer. A few steps later, he turned back and added, "When you've got 'em ready, go over to the outdoor arena and start warmin' up. I'll be there after I swap a few lies with Lane."

Savannah didn't want to go into the arena at first. She kept trying to turn away and at one point, I wondered if she was going to rear up with me. I started doing some "listening warm-ups" right there in front of the gate, bending her, doing turns on the forehand, and jogging small circles, until she started to relax.

When she seemed to be listening to me, I sort of pointed her toward the gate and we did a serpentine through it and into the arena. Once inside, I kept her busy thinking about what *I* wanted rather than giving her time to decide what *she* wanted, or more likely, what she *didn't* want to do.

As I jogged her around the arena, I half expected her to find something to spook at as she passed the bucking chutes that formed the fence line along the eastern edge of the arena. She didn't shy from any of that, so I figured she'd find something scary at the grandstands that ran the length of the west side. Surprisingly, she didn't find anything to cause her to explode there either. Not that she was calm. She was totally tense and tight. But gradually, as I focused on making her be attentive to me, while using the softest hands possible, she started to relax.

Chapter 22 - Ring Sour

By the time Ben got back and called us to take the horses into the covered arena for a look around, Savannah felt like herself. Her new self, I giggled, not her old self.

We walked the horses across the dirt road that separated the two arenas and again, Savannah balked when she got to the gate. I quietly bent her into a circle and worked on her attentiveness again.

"Did she act ring sour at the other arena gate too?" Ben asked.

"If ring sour means she didn't want to go into the arena, then yes," I said. Finally feeling that I had her attention again, I sent her through the gate and into the covered pen.

I kept working her in circles and serpentines all the way around the arena until she was paying attention only to me. There was one spot where a big wooden platform-looking thing was leaned up against the out-side of the fence. She didn't want to go near it at first, but she finally figured out that it wasn't going to hurt her and jogged past without swerving.

When I felt that she was truly listening, I stopped to let her relax, right next to the platform thing.

"Good choice," Ben said from where he stood down by the gate. "Let her rest there for a few minutes, then bring her over here."

Looking around, I noticed that Xender and Violet had taken their horses back to the trailer. I smiled to myself to think that Savannah hadn't got upset when they'd left, but was still willing to listen to me. Two people brought their horses in and were lunging them, working them in a circle around where they stood, using a long rope to control them. Another rider joined us in the arena, too, a little girl on an old, sway-backed horse. As she rode toward me, I realized that she looked familiar.

She was so busy staring at Savannah, she hadn't even noticed me.

"Hi, Emma," I said. "I didn't know you rode horses." Thinking about it, I realized I didn't know much about her outside of school.

She looked up at me in surprise. When she still didn't seem to recognize me, I said, "It's me, Meghan, from P.E. and science class."

Her expression changed from confusion to happiness.

"Meghan!" she said. Then her eyes went back to Savannah and she said, almost dreamily, "She's really a pretty horse."

"Your horse is cute too," I lied. Looking for something I could be honest about, I finally said, "What a pretty tail he has." His tail was long and completely tangle-free. It was definitely his best feature and she must have worked a long time to get it looking so nice.

Emma beamed.

A loud train whistle shattered the quietness of the morning.

Chapter 23
Emma and Skittles

I jumped at the sound. Savannah flinched. And Emma's old horse stood stone-cold still. Seeing Emma's horse so unconcerned probably helped Savannah stay calm, despite what my nerves had done. I looked toward the noise and saw puffs of smoke rising rhythmically over the roof of the long, low barn that ran alongside the covered arena. And I heard the distinctive *chug-chug-chug* of the steam-powered train that is one of Durango's most famous tourist attractions: the Durango-Silverton Narrow Gauge Railroad. I'd ridden the train with my parents the first summer we had lived in the area, and it had been a lot of fun. At the time, I hadn't noticed that the tracks went right past the Durango fairgrounds.

"Your horse is so pretty," Emma said again. "What's her name?"

"Savannah," I answered. "What's your horse's name?"

"Skittles," she told me, petting the old horse fondly on his neck. "I'm going to ride him in the horse show today. I've never been in a horse show before, but Dad says Skittles and I are going to do great! He says there are Novice classes for new show people, and they're just right for me."

"I'll be cheering for you Emma," I told her. Then I dismounted and walked Savannah to the gate where Ben was waiting for us.

"Looks as if you've got yer mare listenin'," Ben said.

"Except for going in and out of the gate, she's been real good," I told him.

"How bad was she when you first tried to go into the big arena? I was over at Lane's trailer when you went in and didn't see if you were having problems right off."

"Oh, she wasn't horrible or anything. But she made it clear she didn't want to go through that gate."

"She's probably rememberin' some bad stuff out of her past," Ben said. "That makes it even more important that you give her a good day today. Jes' keep bein' patient but firm like ya been doin'."

"Did you see her when the train whistle blew?" I bragged.

"Yep. She didn't seem to care too much about that."

"Standing next to Emma's kind old horse probably helped her," I said.

Ben nodded in agreement.

Chapter 23 - Emma and Skittles

We were silent for a long moment, then we both spoke at the same time.

"Meghan—"

"Ben—"

"Go ahead," Ben said. "What did you want to say?"

"Well, I was wondering if I could switch out of the Novice classes into the regular 12 & under division. I told Emma I would be cheering for her, and that's going to be hard to do if I'm competing against her."

Ben laughed. "I was just about to tell you that I signed you up for the 12 & under. Figured you oughta be tryin' to whup up on Xender and Scout, not a sweet little girl like Lane's young'un and her antique horse."

"Thanks, Ben."

"Not that I think beatin' that kid would be easy. Her dad used to show that ol' horse years ago when he was in 4-H, and that was a real nice horse. He didn't look like much even then, but he was smart and willin' and would do whatever Lane asked. And Lane was positively braggin' about what a good hand his little girl is. That kinda amused me because Lane's not the braggin' sort."

Ben turned away from watching Emma, who was jogging Skittles around the arena, and looked at me. "Besides, the way you and Xender been actin' lately, seems like you two need a chance to try to beat each other."

"I thought you said my job today was to give Savannah a good experience? Not to try to beat anyone else."

"Oh, it most definitely is. But if you *do* give her a good ride, *and* she responds the way she's capable of, *and* the judge takes notice, you might manage to get into the ribbons once or twice." He smiled. "But you are absolutely correct. That is not what's important."

We walked back over to the horse trailer where Violet had unsaddled her horse and was cleaning out his feet.

"Pull off yer mare's bridle, loosen her girth, and let her have some hay and water, while you watch Violet compete in Showmanship."

As I tied Savannah to the trailer, I noticed that Violet wasn't cleaning her horse's feet as I'd first thought. She was putting something on them. As she set his foot down, she carefully placed it on a piece of cardboard, to keep it out of the dust and then finished applying the polish down around the edges of his hooves.

Violet glanced up at me. Sounding a lot like her grandfather, she said, "Oh quit gapin' at me. If you don't close your mouth, you're gonna catch flies in it."

"I just, um, never saw anyone put nail polish on a horse before."

"It's not nail polish. It's a concoction Grandpa makes out of onion oil. It shines their hooves up without drying them out. And I hope you saw how I did it because you're going to do that for your horse before the Royalty contest," she informed me as she peeled plastic gloves off her hands. "And you're going to have your nails done too."

I opened my mouth to protest, but she cut me off. "We'll figure out the color once I decide which outfit you're going to wear that day. But right now, put your apron back on and give me a hand."

She shoved a bottle of baby oil in my direction and told me to rub it all over Paint's muzzle. Once I had finished, his muzzle was gleaming and shiny.

"Now rub it on the skin around his eyes. Just make sure you don't get any *in* his eyes. And don't use too much of it. I don't want it on his haircoat."

When I finished, Violet handed me a towel she had dampened with some sort of spray and told me to rub it all over Paint, following the direction that his hair naturally went. While I did that, she put a pretty leather halter and matching lead shank on Paint and then pulled off her apron.

"Hang onto that rag, and when I get to the gate— right before I walk into the arena—you can dust off my boots and fix my jeans."

I looked down and saw that her pant legs were stuffed into the tops of her boots to keep them from dragging on the ground and getting dirty.

As she led Paint toward the arena, Xender popped around the end of the trailer.

"Well, don't you make the perfect servant girl to Queen Violet," he snarked.

"I'm not a servant," I shot back. "I'm a *friend*." After a hesitation, I added, "You should try that sometime."

He turned his back and walked away.

The Free Horse

Chapter 24
Traffic Jam

Ben was leaning on the fence near the in-gate, watching Violet as she walked and trotted Paint in the area in front of the covered arena. She stopped him without even pulling on the lead rope, then turned over his haunches and trotted away again.

"Looks as if she's got her horse listenin' real good," he said, "and he looks mighty fine the way you two gals have him all gussied up."

Good, I thought to myself, if Ben approves, who cares what Xender thinks?

Violet appeared beside me and I dutifully dusted her boots, fixed her pant legs, and then checked to see that there were no other bits of dust on either her or the horse.

When I stepped back, Violet walked grandly into the arena. She and Paint reminded me of the fashion show models I'd seen in video clips. Both looked confident and gorgeous.

As seven other horses were led into the arena, I looked with a critical eye to see which horses were as beautifully groomed as Violet's. To my surprise, they all looked fantastic: shiny, with polished hooves, oiled noses, and pretty halters. But watching them, I couldn't help but feel that Violet and Paint outshone them all.

Ben explained some of the finer points about the way the handlers were supposed to be working their horses. From what I could see, Violet was doing everything right! One other girl looked almost as precise as Violet, but that girl seemed stiff, almost like a toy soldier. I just knew Violet would win.

When the announcer called the toy soldier for first place, I was really disappointed for Violet's sake. She walked out of the arena carrying the second place red ribbon.

Without speaking, she headed back to the trailer.

I started to follow her, but Ben stopped me.

"She gets a mite tart-tongued after gettin' beat in a close contest like that one. I'd stay here an' watch the 12 & under kids compete if I was you."

"Why aren't Savannah and I showing in this class?" I asked.

"I didn't want either you or the mare to have the extra stress. It takes a lot of time and practice to get good at Showmanship, and I'd rather you spent yer time gettin' ready fer the ridin' classes. Then I had to consider that, well, we wouldn't have wanted yer mare to get sweaty before Showmanship, and I wasn't real sure how she'd be behavin' this mornin'. You might've had to get her sweaty."

"But I didn't. Well, not too much anyway," I said proudly. "The only thing that seemed to bother her was going in the gate."

"Yeah," Ben agreed. "Like I said, she's probably recollectin' some bad times when she was younger."

"Then I'm going to do my best to replace those bad memories by making good ones for her today!"

After the ten kids in my age group finished Showmanship and left the arena, Emma followed a woman leading another old horse in through the gate for the Novice class. The older woman won the class and walked out not only with the blue ribbon but with a huge smile. Her smile, however, paled in comparison to the one on Emma's face. Emma positively glowed as she hung her red ribbon on Skittles' halter and proudly hugged him around his saggy old neck.

I shouted my congratulations to Emma, trying to sound sincere, which was a little difficult since she had placed last out of two. But Emma was happy, and that's all that mattered. Then I hurried back to the horse trailer to get Savannah ready for her first class, Western Pleasure.

I warmed her up by jogging some circles, then got back to the in-gate in time to see the very end of Violet's Western Pleasure class. Violet rode out with a yellow, third place ribbon and a compliment from her Grandpa.

"You gave Paint a nice ride."

I couldn't hear if Violet said anything in response, but for a brief second, I saw a small smile appear on her face.

Walking toward the arena, Savannah slowed to a stop and started to back away from the gate. I sat back, turned her head slightly and pushed her forward with my legs and seat, which stopped her backing attitude.

Before she could resist again, other horses began walking past her. She must have decided there's safety in numbers, so she went on in with them.

Once in the arena, she was really good, listening to my cues and doing whatever I asked. I was thinking about how proud I was of her when I suddenly became aware of the fact that we were loping along in the middle of a traffic jam, with three or four horses right in front of us and two more on either side. I had allowed us to get boxed in, which Ben had warned me not to do.

Just then, the rider ahead of us, having realized her horse was on the wrong lead, abruptly pulled her horse back to a jog. As that horse slowed, Savannah was forced back to a jog also, breaking gait right in front of the judge.

I slowed her more to let the others get ahead of us and then put her back into a lope, but the judge had seen our mistake. For the rest of the class, I concentrated not only on riding Savannah correctly, but on keeping her out of heavy traffic. Ben had cautioned me many times during lessons over the previous few weeks about getting trapped. He had even told me how to prevent it. By going deeper into some corners and cutting other corners, I found that, just as he'd said, I could keep Savannah away from the horses whose riders were letting them get bunched up.

After the rail work, the judge had us line our horses up in the middle of the arena and, one at a time, asked us to back up. Then the ring steward took the judge's score sheet to the announcer, who read the results. When Xender's name was called for fourth place, he pulled his cowboy hat off his head in a surprising show of gentlemanly manners and walked over to collect his white ribbon from the woman who was in charge of handing out the prizes. After the sixth and final placing was announced, I dismounted, as Ben had recommended, and led my mare out of the arena.

"Oh, Ben," I said as he met me at the gate, "I'm so sorry. I really messed that up."

"The way I see it, you did a fine job of givin' yer little mare a pleasant ride, and you had yerself a good learnin' experience about stayin' outta traffic. I'd say you got yer money's worth out of that class."

I took a deep breath of relief. Hearing Ben say that meant a lot.

Handing me a sheet of paper, Ben said, "Here's the pattern fer yer next class. Memorize it, and if you've got any questions, ask me or Violet or Xender." Ben chuckled. "If you can get anywhere near Xender, that is."

Xender was sitting on Scout, completely surrounded by a group of giggling girls on their own horses.

I started giggling too.

Violet walked up just then and looked in the same direction as Ben and me. Even she started laughing. "Xender's a babe magnet. Who knew?"

"You two save yer tormentin' of the poor kid 'til we get home. Right now, you need to be learnin' yer pattern for Horsemanship."

"This is the sort of thing we'll have to do at the Royalty contest," Violet said, taking the paper out of my hand to study it. "It's all about precision. All the riders in the class are capable of making their horses jog, lope, turn, and back up. But to do well in this class you're going to need to do the pattern exactly as it's shown and with the least amount of visible effort."

Violet handed it back to me. "Do you understand what you'll need to do?"

"I think so— *All right!!*" I shouted at the top of my lungs, as Emma and Skittles were announced as first place winners in the Novice Pleasure class. Then, in an attempt to be polite, I clapped for the woman who got second place too. Emma rode out of the arena smiling and hugging Skittles around the neck. The woman rode out looking annoyed.

Violet turned and mounted her horse. "Watch me in my class. We're doing the same pattern."

I watched.

It was beautiful. Violet's posture was perfect and her aids practically invisible as she guided Paint through the class. Several of the girls who had beaten her earlier had nice goes too. But it was Violet who walked out with the blue ribbon this time.

The announcer called my class into the arena.

The Free Horse

Chapter 25
Patterns

All of the entries in my class were asked to enter and line up at one end of the arena. Savannah wasn't quite as sticky about going through the gate this time. As we joined the lineup, I heard Xender's number called to go first. I studied his ride and was proud, for Ben's sake, to see how nice it looked. Like Violet, he sat straight and tall, with a correct lower leg. Also like Violet, his pattern was precise, with minimal visible aids. But suddenly I realized he had not done one of the maneuvers. Where he was supposed to stop and back up for five steps before proceeding at a lope, he had only stopped. He hadn't backed up at all. He finished his pattern as nicely as he had started it. Except for the missing backup, it had been excellent.

They called the next exhibitor's number. She went out and did the same pattern as Xender's, but not nearly as smoothly. She, too, only stopped and didn't back up where she was supposed to. The next rider did the same. Now I started to worry. Was the pattern different between the two age groups? No. Ben would have mentioned it. And Violet did actually tell me to watch her class because it was exactly the same. Taking a deep breath, I made my decision.

When they called my number next, I felt ready to go. I squeezed lightly with my legs. For a fraction of a second, Savannah's ears flattened and she balked at going forward. I quietly clucked to her with my voice and squeezed a little harder with my legs. To my relief, she stepped forward, ears up, all trace of resistance gone.

I focused all of my thoughts on quietly asking her to do the pattern and she responded like a dream. Everything from her jogging circles to her stop, her five backing steps, and her canter departs were just what I asked for. I wanted to fall on her neck and hug her the way Emma had hugged Skittles, but I knew from Ben's coaching that I wasn't allowed to do that in the show ring when the class was going on. So instead, I rode her back into the lineup to sit and wait. About half of the remaining contestants included the backing steps in their pattern. The rest did not. I wasn't sure who was correct, Xender or me. Or I wasn't until they announced the placings, and I learned that we had placed third! At that point, I did fall on Savannah's neck with a huge hug! As I straightened, the judge walked over to me.

"I'd like to have pinned you higher, miss," she said, because you rode that pattern beautifully and your horse was wonderfully responsive." She patted Savannah on the neck. "But I'm afraid you just don't fit this horse. You're too tall for her. It's just not a good match."

I wasn't sure what to say, so I finally managed a thank you.

She started to walk away, then turned back and said, "I hope you realize I'm not trying to be unkind here. But you're too good a rider and she's too nice a horse, and the reality is, well, you both need to move on to another partner."

I collected Savannah's yellow ribbon and rode out to meet Ben. Emma congratulated me as we passed each other at the gate.

Violet stated flatly, "You should have won," before riding over toward the other arena, where the Trail class had begun.

Even Xender rode over and said, "Congratulations," which was the first nice thing he'd said in about a week.

"How did you place?" I asked.

He turned his horse and rode away without saying anything.

Ben looked at me kind of funny.

"The judge stopped to talk with me right after they announced my name, so I didn't hear the rest of the placings," I explained.

"Well, ya don't generally place when ya bust the pattern. And this judge knows what she's lookin' fer. So he didn't place."

"He and Scout looked good though," I said.

"Lookin' good don't matter much if ya can't get yer pattern right," Ben said. "He was too busy chattin' with his fan club to focus on what he should have. And it bit him. Be interestin' to see how he does with the Reinin' pattern."

"Am I in that too?" I asked. "I haven't learned that one yet."

"Nope. I didn't want to push this little mare too hard, so I didn't enter you in that class. Yer last class is the Trail, and you can ride on over and do that one whenever you've got a mind to. There's a different judge fer that class and no draw order. I think Violet went over a couple o' minutes ago if you want to go watch her. But take notice: there may be some differences in the trail course between her age group and yours. I haven't looked yet."

Emma's Horsemanship class had been in the arena while Ben and I talked. "Hold up a minute," he said. "I think our little friend is about to win herself another class."

The microphone crackled on, and Emma was indeed named the winner. Ben and I shouted and clapped for the very happy little girl, and then applauded encouragingly for the grumpy older woman who'd been bested again.

Chapter 25 - Patterns

I led Savannah over to the other arena just in time to watch Violet ride Paint in the gate for the Trail class. She picked up a jog and weaved back and forth between a series of cones that were set up in a line. At the end of the cones, she stopped and side-passed Paint over a pole on the ground, then bent down, retrieved an envelope from a mailbox that was nailed to the top of a post, waved it at the judge, and stuck it back into the box. She side-passed Paint back over the pole and then stepped off into a lope. Stopping between two barrels, she picked up a sack full of cans from the top of the right-hand barrel, lifted it across in front of the saddle horn, and set it down on the one to her left.

From there, Violet walked off a few steps, dismounted, dropped her reins in the dirt, and walked back to the two barrels, where she put the bag of cans back on top the first barrel. Returning to Paint, who hadn't budged, she picked up her reins and mounted back up. She turned and walked him over to where a rope was strung between two vertical posts. Unhooking the rope at one end, she held it aside while she walked Paint between the posts and then hooked the rope back up. From there, she jogged to two poles on the ground, stopped, and backed Paint between them. Turning toward the arena gate, she rode Paint across a wooden platform—the one I'd seen propped up against the fence this morning—and then left the arena.

"That looked like fun!" I told Violet.

She just said, "Good luck." And then rode away, calling back over her shoulder, "I have to go get ready for Reining."

The only two things I was concerned about were crossing the wooden platform that Savannah had shied from earlier and having to dismount and walk away. As much as we'd worked on "join-up" work in the round pen, I was pretty sure Savannah would follow me instead of ground tying as she was supposed to. I looked at the piece of cardboard nailed up beside the in-gate where the trail course was drawn out by hand. It showed everything exactly as Violet had done it. Then I noticed that there was an asterisk at the two barrels, saying that the 12 & under and Novice riders just had to pick the bag of cans up and then set it back down on the *same* barrel. A second asterisk noted that we didn't have to ground tie either. That was a relief! It also showed that the rope between the two posts that we had to unhook and go through was called a gate, and the wooden platform was called a bridge.

I went over the pattern in my head several times to make sure I knew it. I walked to an open area to stop and back up and do a couple of turns on the forehand, just to make sure Savannah was listening. Then we returned to the Trail arena to start our course.

Savannah slowed as she approached the gate, but I sat back a little and pushed with my seat, keeping leg pressure on both sides of her body, and she walked into the arena with only a slight hesitation. Once in the show pen, she was all business, going through each obstacle just as I asked. Even the bridge wasn't scary now that it was lying on the ground where it belonged.

Emma and the woman from the Novice class were waiting their turns when I rode out.

"Ohhhh, that was really pretty," Emma said to me. Since we were talking, the other woman rode in ahead of Emma to ride the course. To be honest, she made a real mess of it, despite the fact that her instructor was leaning on the rail and shouting instructions. After the judge picked up the bag of cans from where she'd dropped them, put the rope gate back into place, reset the back-through poles, and set up the two cones she'd knocked over, it was Emma's turn. Other than getting tangled up with the rope gate and finally dropping it and stepping off the side of the bridge when she was halfway across, Emma and Skittles had a nice go, making it apparent that she would add another blue ribbon to her Novice collection.

Emma's Dad hugged her when she rode out of the arena. Then he turned to me.

"Congratulations on *your* nice ride," he said. "Ben has told me what a challenge this little horse was when you first got her. Seeing how well you're doing with her today has really gotta be making him proud."

I thanked him before turning away quickly, my eyes suddenly brimming with tears.

The Free Horse

Chapter 26
Horse for Sale?

So many emotions were bubbling up inside me that I wasn't sure if my tears were ones of joy for how well Savannah had done, or if they were from hurt from the judge's comments earlier about Savannah and me not being a good match, or maybe from hearing Mr. Nelson refer to her as the "little horse," the way everyone did.

I trudged back to the horse trailer to unsaddle, water, and brush her. While filling the hay bag for her, I heard the announcer say that Violet had won her Reining class.

Leaving Savannah contentedly munching on hay, I walked back over to the arena in time to see Xender run his Reining pattern. It looked good to me. And from Ben's reaction, it was clear he had stayed on pattern this time. In fact, he won the class over the seven other 12 & under riders who had competed.

"Congratulations!" I had time to tell him as he rode out with his blue ribbon, right before he was engulfed by the gaggle of girls who had followed him around all day.

A few minutes later the announcer said he had the results for the Trail as well as the names of the Division Champions.

Violet had won the Trail, which also clinched the championship for the 13 to 18 division. Xender won the 12 & under Trail on Scout, and Savannah and I placed second! And of course, Emma and Skittles not only won Trail but were also the champions in the Novice division!

Walking back with my red ribbon from Trail, I saw Ben and Mr. Nelson, whose backs were toward me, talking.

"I can see why Emma is so fond of that young lady who rides with you. She's a real nice girl. A good hand too. You've gotta be proud of how she handled that little mare of hers today."

I turned away embarrassed and feeling like an eavesdropper. Besides, I didn't want to hear the words "little mare" again. Walking back to the horse trailer, I was surprised to see two women standing next to Savannah.

"I told you she wasn't too small for you. She just looks small with that girl riding her."

I recognized the one gal right away as the person who had shown in the Novice division against Emma. Then I realized the woman speaking was the one who had been coaching her through the Trail class.

Chapter 26 - Horse for Sale?

"Speaking of— Here she is now. Do you own this horse, or does she belong to Ben?" the woman asked.

"She's my horse," I said.

"Then you're the person I want to talk to," the woman smiled, though it didn't seem like a real smile because the hard look in her eyes hadn't changed a bit.

"My client here is in the market for a new horse," she said, "having progressed about as far as her current horse will allow her. And since it's clear that you, too, are ready to move, um, *up* to another horse, I thought you might be interested in selling this little mare."

I felt my mouth open and then close again. I didn't know what to say. Before I could open it again, Ben's voice came from somewhere behind me, "Would you like me to handle this fer you, Meghan?"

"Sure, Ben," I answered gratefully. I hadn't heard him walk up and wasn't certain how long he'd been standing there or how much he'd heard. But it must've been enough because he launched into his sales pitch like some slick horse trader.

"She's a quality mare, ladies, as you clearly saw today. This was Meghan's first time in the show pen, but they did well, even against all the seasoned horses they were up against."

What was Ben doing? Was he actually trying to sell my horse out from under me?!

"Now of course, the little mare doesn't actually belong to Meghan, but to her folks, who, unfortunately, couldn't be here today. But I think they might be convinced to consider selling her for a very reasonable price."

What was he saying?!

"I'd be happy to present them with yer offer of, say…"

The dollar amount that floated off his tongue at the end of that sentence positively stunned me. My parents could have bought a really nice new car for that much money.

If Ben expected the two women to agree to his outrageous price, he was sadly mistaken. They exchanged glances, thanked him for his time, and said they'd get back to him. They took one last look at Savannah and walked away.

Violet and Xender led their horses back to the trailer just then.

"Get yer horses unsaddled so we can load 'em up and head fer home. We've got more horses to ride and some chores waitin' for us," he said.

It wasn't until we were all in the cab of the truck and pulling out of the fairgrounds that he started to laugh.

"I was scared there for a minute that I hadn't priced yer little mare high enough and that the ol' gal was goin' to pull out her wallet and start peelin' off wads of cash fer a down payment."

Totally confused, I asked, "Why did you tell them she was for sale?"

Chapter 26 - Horse for Sale?

Still chuckling, he answered, "When someone offers to buy a horse that you don't want to sell, always put a price on 'em. Jes' make the price too big. Big enough that they're not goin' to be fool enough to pay it."

"Why not just tell them the horse isn't for sale?" I asked.

"'Cause if you do that, they'll jes' keep pesterin' ya. A big, inflated price tag saves everyone time an' aggravation."

"But Ben," I asked, "do you think I *should* be thinking about selling her?" I told him about the judge's comments after the horsemanship class.

"Well, I wouldn't sell her to that lady no matter what. She's not a good enough rider to handle yer little, um, yer mare."

"Yeah," Xender said. "Did you see her ripping on her horse's mouth after her lousy ride in the Horsemanship? She took out her lack of skills on that poor horse."

"I'm afraid I did, Xender. If that had been one of my students actin' like that to a horse, I'd have—" Ben stopped. "Well, I don't know what I'd have done fer sure. I jes' know that person would've learned a valuable lesson about good horsemanship real quick-like."

"I'll bet they would!" Xender laughed.

"Of course now, if they had jes' gone off course in their class, I probably wouldn't be quite so riled up. But I still wouldn't be real happy," Ben said.

Xender turned red.

"I'm sorry, Grandpa. That was really stupid. I must have explained that pattern to a half dozen other riders—"

"All girls!" Violet pointed out.

Xender got even redder.

"But somehow, when I was doing the pattern myself, I just plain forgot that one part."

"It's all about where your focus is during the class," Violet chided him.

"Well, *you* only got it right because there were no boys around to distract you."

Violet actually laughed. "That's why horse shows are so easy. No distractions! Looks as if they're about to start getting a lot tougher for my baby brother though. All those cute girls seem to find him *irresistible*! Even some of the girls from my age group were circling you like bees to honey."

Violet and I both dissolved into laughter, while Xender's face and ears turned redder still.

I hadn't really thought about it, but Xender *had* been the only guy showing a horse there. It also occurred to me that the girls surrounding him had all been prettily made up. If he could put up with them, he could get used to my new look too.

Chapter 27
Wasps

"Look how good Savannah is being!" I shouted out to Xender as he walked past the arena toward the barn. "I've been riding her for at least half an hour with no one else around and she's been fantastic! She couldn't have done so well a month ago."

Xender had walked up to the fence and was staring at me with an odd look on his face. "Yeah, well, a *lot* has changed in the past month," he grumbled before turning and walking away.

"What's that supposed to mean?" I asked toward his retreating back. "Just 'cause my looks have changed a little doesn't mean *I've* changed."

He just shook his head and kept walking.

"Come on, girl," I said, patting Savannah on her shiny, golden neck. "Let's get out of here before he gets back. I don't want to put up with him if he's going to keep being such a twerp." I rode to the gate, opened it and walked through, turning Savannah toward the trail along the river.

Even this early in the morning, the August sun was beating down, making me sweat under my riding helmet. A droplet ran down my forehead, and I quickly wiped it away. I would have to remember to check my mascara when I got back from my ride and make sure I didn't have raccoon eyes.

It felt good to get into the shade of the cottonwood trees that lined this stretch of the river. But that didn't cool my annoyance.

"Why's he being such an obnoxious jerk, Savannah? He acts as if it's some horrible thing that I'm friends with his sister now and that I'm taking more care with how I look. I mean, seriously? What is his problem? It's okay for *him* to have all the good-looking girls chasing after him at the horse show but *I'm* not supposed to try to look nice?"

I looked at the crystal clear water flowing past us and took a deep breath. "But I don't want to talk about stupid stuff on such a beautiful day when I'm riding my beautiful mare along a beautiful river! I'm not going to let Xender's crummy attitude ruin this for me. Let's talk about something else, like how perfect you're going to be when we go try out at the Rodeo Royalty contest! We're going to show those judges the best pattern they've ever seen. Violet says I should practice visualizing our test, doing every step of it perfectly, and, oh Savannah, I really can see it all in my head. You're going to be as shiny as a gold coin. And your mane and tail will be all silky and white after I've bathed you and used conditioner on them. And I'll polish the silver conchos on my saddle until they sparkle. And I'll even—"

A rabbit jumped out from behind a clump of bunch grass, startling Savannah, who flinched in surprise. I started giggling. "You used to get a whole lot more excited about things like that, Savannah. Look at you. You're walking all relaxed as if you've already forgotten that silly rabbit. What a good girl you are."

A ring-necked pheasant flew up in front of her less than a mile later. Once again, she barely flinched. I bent down and hugged her around her neck.

It was time to turn around. Most of the ride back to the barn was uneventful, but as we approached the pasture, Savannah heard one of the ranch horses whinny. Her head went up, and she broke into a trot. I immediately stopped her and backed her up. Then I made her stand still before allowing her to walk toward the barn again. She got the message and walked quietly. "Good girl," I praised her.

I was really proud of her great behavior all morning, and I wanted to share that with someone else, but Ben was gone to town and Xender was being a grump. Maybe Violet would be at the barn when I got back.

She wasn't. Xender wasn't there either, which was fine with me.

I put Savannah back out in the field and sat down in the shade of the barn to clean my saddle. Only three more days until the Royalty Contest.

It was less than twenty miles to the fairgrounds just east of Cortez where the Royalty Contest was supposed to start at ten, so Violet and I had time to bathe the horses and apply their hoof polish before we left the ranch that morning. When we arrived at the fairgrounds, we unloaded the horses from the trailer, tacked them up, and were soon in the arena, warming up. Savannah hesitated at the gate, but only for a second.

"Good girl," I told her, rubbing her on her neck.

As we jogged around the far end of the arena, I suddenly heard a crashing sound and a girl's screams coming from the far side of a horse trailer.

Violet rode up beside me. Her eyes looked huge.

As the racket continued, I handed my reins to Violet, bailed off my horse, jumped over the arena fence, and ran toward whatever was happening. I slowed as I approached the trailer and gave it some space as I rounded the end.

In a cloud of dust, I saw a horse down on the ground, his hind legs under the trailer, his head up in the air, suspended from where his halter was tied to the side of the trailer.

I heard Ben's voice yelling, "Stay back! Give him some room so he can stand back up without steppin' on you!" But Ben wasn't talking to me. A petite, blonde-headed girl was edging toward the horse.

With two big steps, I caught up with her, grabbed her around the shoulders and pulled her back to safety. She turned and looked up at me in confusion.

"It's me. It's Meghan," I told her in my calmest voice. "We need to stand back so we don't get in Skittles' way while he stands back up."

The look in her eyes changed to one of recognition. "Skittles is hurt," she told me in a quavery voice.

"I know, Emma, but we need to stay back out of the way and let Ben and your dad help him." I took her by the hand and led her further away from the struggling horse. She followed me, but kept watching back over her shoulder.

Ben jumped onto the edge of the horse trailer and clinging precariously to it, reached in and began sawing on the lead rope with his pocket knife. "Look out!" he warned as Skittles thrashed around even harder. As the rope gave way, the frightened horse was finally able to maneuver into position to free himself. Within a minute, he managed to get his legs out from under the trailer and lurch to his feet.

Emma pointed to Skittles' legs, where flaps of skin hung down and blood pumped out. "Skittles is hurt," Emma said again and started to cry.

Emma's dad jerked open the tack compartment door, grabbed a towel, tore it in half, and handed a piece to Ben. Both men bent down and pressed the cloth against the worst of the cuts in an attempt to stanch the flow of blood.

Ben looked up at me and said, "How about if you take Emma over to the arena and, uh, quiz her about rodeo events?"

"Sure, Ben," I said, gently turning the crying girl away from her injured horse and leading her over to where Violet still stood holding Savannah.

Tears continued to run down Emma's face.

Violet was staring at us questioningly.

"Emma's horse had, um, a little problem," I said, "so while Ben and her dad take care of him, Emma's going to hang out with us."

Turning to Emma, I said, "This is my friend Violet. She knows a lot about rodeo. She was the Junior Queen Attendant this past year."

"I like rodeos," Emma sniffed. "I want to be the Rodeo Princess. But Skittles is hurt. Some wasps stung him. They tried to get me, too, but I ran away. When Skittles tried to run, he fell down and got stuck." The tears, which had temporarily stopped, resumed in a big way.

"Ben and your dad will help Skittles." I tried to reassure her while I searched my pockets for a tissue to help dry her eyes and nose.

"Dad loves Skittles too," she said between sobs.

"Do you like paint horses, Emma?" I asked, trying to distract her. "Isn't that a handsome paint horse Violet's riding? Do you remember him from the horse show a few weeks ago?"

"I remember. He's nice." Then she pointed to Savannah. "But she is *really* pretty."

"Do you know what color she is?" I asked.

"She's a palomino," Emma responded. "I've seen pictures of palominos. She's even prettier than the pictures."

"Thank you, Emma. That's sweet of you to say."

"Can I ride her? Please?"

The Free Horse

Chapter 28
She Likes Me

Violet and I exchanged looks. Emma's request to ride Savannah scared us both. But we needed to keep her distracted.

"Um, sure," I finally said. I shortened the stirrups on my saddle as far as they would go and helped her up onto Savannah's back, all while keeping a firm hold on the reins.

As soon as I started leading Savannah around the arena, Emma's tears were gone, replaced by a big smile.

"Can I ride Savannah by myself?" Emma asked. "She likes me."

"Uh, let me walk with you awhile longer," I said.

A few minutes later, Emma pointed, "Uh oh. Look! If a horse steps on that, he'll hurt his foot."

I followed her line of sight and saw a ragged, rusty chunk of metal sticking out of the arena dirt. Leading

Savannah over to it, I bent down and grabbed it with my free hand, but it was stuck. With two hands, I was pretty sure I could get it out and, after a brief struggle, I did. But when I turned back to show Emma, she and Savannah were fifty feet away at a jog.

I tossed the metal over the fence and started walking after them, calling out as calmly as possible, "You're okay, Emma. Just say, 'Whoa' and lift the reins a little bit and Savannah will stop for you."

"This is fun!" Emma said. Then she repeated, "Savannah likes me."

If I ran to Savannah, I was afraid she might shy away from me and dump Emma, so all I could do was walk, quickly and quietly, after them.

Violet saw my predicament and cut across the arena to try to intercept the pair.

But Emma sat back, squeezed with her legs, and put Savannah into a lope. Violet pulled up, not wanting to risk an unintended horse race.

Emma's smile could not have been any bigger. Savannah was loping along steadily, her ears cocked back toward her rider, listening attentively. Emma was guiding Savannah through a series of stops, turns, and circles when it finally occurred to me: she was practicing the pattern for today's competition! Once I realized that, I was able to anticipate where her next stop would be. I got into position and managed to catch Savannah's reins as she finished her pattern the third time.

Chapter 28 - She Likes Me

"That was really good, Emma," I said out loud, while my internal monologue added, "especially since Savannah didn't kill you!"

"She likes me," Emma insisted again. "She wants to do the pattern with me."

I thought about that for a minute. "That would be okay with me, if it's okay with your dad. We'll ask him, as soon as he and Ben get done taking care of Skittles."

At the mention of her poor injured horse, tears welled up in her eyes again.

Looking for a new distraction, I asked her if my saddle was comfortable for her.

"It's nice," she said, "but I like my own saddle best."

"Okay, then let's take Savannah back to Ben's horse trailer and take my saddle off of her. Then while you brush her, I'll go get your saddle and bring it over to see if it fits her," I suggested.

"Okay," she said as I started leading Savannah toward the gate. "You don't need to hold her, Meghan," Emma told me. "Savannah likes me. She'll be good."

Reluctantly, I dropped my hand back down to my side but stayed within grabbing distance as we walked toward the trailer.

When I asked Violet to hang out with Emma while I went for the saddle, she volunteered to go get it herself. Emma and I pulled my saddle off the mare's back, and I carefully put it back into the trailer to keep it clean. We brushed Savannah's already-gleaming coat. Then Emma began to pick through the hairs of Savannah's silky tail to make it look pretty and full without accidentally pulling any hairs out of it.

Soon Violet was back, leading her paint horse with Emma's saddle propped up on top of her own saddle. "Grandpa will be over in a few minutes. He has, um, concerns."

While we resaddled Savannah, Violet quizzed Emma and me about rodeo, asking us the kinds of questions we'd have to answer later today.

"Wow, Emma, you're going to do great in the interviews!" Violet told her.

Emma beamed in delight. "I like rodeo. Dad and I watch it on television every chance we get."

Once Emma's saddle was on Savannah and the girth was tightened, I offered to help her get back on the horse.

"I can do it myself," she said confidently. With that, she led Savannah over to the arena, climbed up on top of the fence and stepped over into the saddle. Savannah never budged. Violet and I looked at each other in amazement.

Emma rode back into the arena and practiced her pattern again. When she was about halfway through it, I noticed that Emma's dad and Ben were leaning on the fence halfway down the arena, watching her. When she finished, both men applauded. Then they climbed over the fence and walked with Emma back to the gate where Violet and I were standing.

Mr. Nelson asked, "Do I understand correctly that you're going to let Emma ride your horse in the competition today?"

"Yes, sir. If that's okay with you."

Emma piped up, "Savannah really likes me, Dad. She likes doing the pattern too."

Ben smiled. "I believe she truly does like you, Emma. You two look real fine together."

Many of the other girls had arrived and were heading into the arena to warm their horses up. "Let's go tie our horses away from all the dust they're kicking up," Violet said. "Then you come with Meghan and me, and we'll all do some touch-up work on our makeup and hair."

Emma frowned. "I don't have any makeup."

"We'll share," Violet promised.

The Free Horse

Chapter 29
And the Winner is...

While Violet finished her artistry with Emma's makeup, I slipped away and walked over to the announcer's booth where the judges and officials were gathering. "I'm not sure who I should ask, but I have a question," I said when one of them noticed me standing there.

"What's that?" the man asked.

"Well, Emma Nelson's horse got hurt this morning, so I offered to let her ride my mare in the Horsemanship contest. But after she rides, I'll need time to switch saddles," I said. "Is that going to be a problem?"

"We can probably allow a couple of minutes for a tack change," he said kindly.

But a woman behind him turned around just then and said, "Wait a minute, Paul. There's a one-horse, one-rider rule. Sorry, honey, but you can't both compete on the same horse. You're going to have to tell the other girl she's out of luck."

I suddenly felt a lot like I had when I'd gotten the wind knocked out of me. How could I break Emma's heart like that? But then, my own heart wasn't feeling too good either. I'd been working hard for months, looking forward to today and this contest. The only reason Emma was getting along so well with Savannah was because of all the hard work I had put into the mare, with all the bruises that had gone along with it.

By the time I got back to the trailer, Emma had climbed back up on Savannah and was riding into the arena while Ben and her dad looked on.

"She's ridden all her life," Mr. Nelson was telling Ben. "She's real quiet around the horses, and they really do seem to like her and, well, sorta look out for her."

"I can see that," Ben said. "And I gotta tell ya, Lane, you and that old horse of yours have done a real good job of makin' a rider out of her. She's got nice quiet hands. This little yellow mare wouldn't take kindly to her if she didn't."

"Well, clearly the mare has had some excellent training to be as soft and kind as she's being," Mr. Nelson said.

"Yes she has," Ben said, with pride in his voice. "Meghan has done a fine job with her. It's too bad the girl is growin' so fast. After all her work, she's gonna have to sell the mare before long and get herself somethin' more appropriate to her height."

I turned and walked away. Violet's going to shoot me, I thought, wiping tears and mascara from my eyes.

Chapter 29 - And the Winner is...

Emma and Savannah's ride in the Horsemanship pattern was flawless. She rode out of the arena petting the mare's neck and talking to her nonstop, exactly the way I would have.

When she was done, Mr. Nelson started to help her down, explaining that we had to get the saddles switched.

"No we don't," I said.

"Well, I don't think you'll fit into this little pixie's saddle," Ben chuckled.

"I don't need to."

They both turned and looked at me.

"I'm not competing. I can't. There's a one-horse, one-rider rule."

"You should have told us," Mr. Nelson said. "Ben, you go ahead and change the saddle and I'll go tell them there was a mistake."

"No! You can't!" I said. "I already pulled out of the competition. When I told them my decision, they said I'd better be sure, because if I rode into the arena to compete on the same horse Emma rode, we'd both be disqualified. Well, I *was* sure. So that's that. Now let's go watch Violet. She's at the in-gate and she's up next."

Violet's pattern was really good too.

Violet and Emma both did well in the interviews and by day's end, they were named Junior Queen and Princess. They would be riding in the parades between now and next year's rodeo, and they would be representatives of the rodeo at the county fair and the library and the Rotary Club meeting and wherever else they were invited. They would be the ones carrying flags during the Grand Entry and moving steers out of the arena after the Steer Wrestling.

I'd be staying home.

Mom and Dad were both waiting for us at Ben's when we got back to the ranch.

"Oh Meghan, we were so sorry to get your text that you weren't going to be able to compete this morning. She's not hurt badly is she?" Mom asked. "I wanted to come to the fairgrounds to check, but you made it pretty clear that I shouldn't."

"I'm glad you didn't come, Mom. You too, Dad." I said. "Savannah's not the horse that got hurt."

"Well then why didn't you get to compete? We both had arranged to take a few hours off work and come watch! We'd have been there for you," Dad said.

I explained.

They both got the dorky Proud Parent look on their faces, followed by a look of relief that they wouldn't be getting a big vet bill for dealing with an injured horse.

Chapter 30
For All Concerned

The next morning, while I was cleaning pens, Xender surprised me by coming into the pen and working alongside me.

"That was a nice thing you did for Emma," he sort of mumbled.

"Thanks."

We worked in silence for awhile.

"I thought you were turning into a snob like my sister."

"Your sister's not a snob," I said. "She just has different interests than we do."

More shoveling. More silence.

After we finished cleaning all the pens, he grabbed the wheelbarrow and took it over to the manure heap to dump it. While he was busy with that, I sneaked around the side of the barn and grabbed the hose. He didn't see me in time when he was coming back, so the blast of water was a total surprise.

A few minutes later we were sitting in front of the barn in the grass, laughing and drying out.

"Maybe you haven't changed all that much," he admitted.

We heard a truck and trailer coming up the driveway and looked up to see Emma waving happily from the passenger seat. As soon as it stopped, Emma jumped out and ran over to us. She plopped down next to me and gave me a big hug, after which she pulled back a little bit and exclaimed, "You're all wet!"

"Yeah, I dumped a water bucket on her," Xender said.

Seeing Emma's disapproving look, I said, "It's okay, Emma. I started it. I sprayed him with a hose first. It was a game."

Mr. Nelson parked the truck and trailer out of the way and ambled over to join us. "Has Emma asked you her all-important question?"

Emma looked down at her hands, then up at me, then back at her hands. Finally, she said, "I really like Savannah, and she really likes me. And I can't ride Skittles any more because he's hurt and Dad says he's retarded now. Except that's not a very nice word and I told Dad that, but he still says Skittles is retarded."

Mr. Nelson gently corrected her. "What I said was that Skittles is *retired*. That means he's not going to be working anymore, Emma. Now go ahead and ask Meghan your question."

She looked up at me again and blurted out, "Can I please have Savannah? Please!"

"Would you be willing to sell her to us?" Mr. Nelson clarified. "Emma is going to need a horse to ride as the Rodeo Princess, and we think that little mare would be just perfect."

"I, um, I…" I managed to say, before stumbling to a complete stop.

"I know this is probably a hard decision to make, so let me tell you a few things, Meghan. Ben already told us about the mare's background and how difficult she was at first. He told us how hard you've worked to get her where she is today. He also said he was planning to suggest that you sell her and get yourself a bigger horse. And, well, if you *do* decide to sell her, we'd like to be the first ones in line."

"Uh…"

"You probably will want to talk to your parents first," he said. "But if you'll consider it, we sure would be grateful."

"Can I have her, Meghan? Please?" Emma implored.

Ben rode over toward us on the colt he'd been working out in the arena. "Meghan, can I talk with you for a minute? Over here?"

"Sure, Ben." I jumped up and jogged over to him.

He stepped down off his horse and started quietly. "You've done a wonderful job with that little mare, and you've learned a whole lot from her, but it's time to move on. You've got a chance to give the mare a good, life-long home with a family that will love her and take good care of her."

I nodded, but couldn't bring myself to speak.

"I know what they're prepared to offer for her and it's a fair price in exchange for all the time and money you and your folks have invested in her. So here's what I think you should do: Offer 'em the opportunity to take Savannah home and try her out for a week. If they're still sure they want her, they can buy her as long as yer folks agree to the price." He chuckled. "And I'm pretty certain they will."

"But I'll be horseless again!" I nearly cried.

"Not for long, you won't," Ben assured me. "And in the meantime, you can ride Freckles for me every day, starting now. In fact, as soon as you've helped them load Savannah into their trailer, how 'bout if you go catch him and meet me out in the arena?"

I looked out toward the pasture where Savannah was grazing. Then I looked back at Emma, who was nearly dancing up and down with anticipation.

"It's the right thing for all concerned," Ben said.

And with that, Savannah was gone from my life. Just a memory, like Rowdy.

Chapter 30 - For All Concerned

Freckles was even more fun to ride that afternoon than he'd been earlier in the summer. Ben said my hands had improved a lot from riding Savannah, and Freckles had learned a lot as Ben had continued his training. It turned out to be a really fun week. Even so, Freckles was a training horse. He belonged to somebody else.

By week's end, Mr. Nelson showed up at our house to pay my parents for Savannah. Ben had stopped by too, to bring us an AQHA transfer form. I signed the form and handed him her registration papers, which I'd only gotten from the American Quarter Horse Association a few weeks ago myself.

"Emma and that little mare are doing great together," Mr. Nelson told us. "I can't thank you enough!"

"I'm glad Emma's happy," I told him, meaning it. "And it's nice to know that Savannah has such a good home."

"We've had Skittles in the family for twenty-nine years," Mr. Nelson said. "We don't sell the good ones. We just retire them when the time comes."

"Is Skittles healing up okay?" I asked him.

"He's still limping a little, but he should be okay. Emma is taking good care of him, even though it's hard for her to spend much time away from that little palomino!"

After Mr. Nelson left, Ben put another transfer form and another set of registration papers on the table. "While you're signin' things, how about if we fill this out too?"

181

"What's this for?" I asked, suddenly noticing the funny grins on Ben's and my parents' faces.

"Well, sweetie, as you know, your mother and I never especially enjoyed owning a free horse." Dad paused for dramatic effect. "So we decided we should *buy* you one!"

I read the name on the registration papers. "Royal Hank Freckles." I looked up at Ben. "Freckles? Your training horse? Freckles?"

"Actually, he hasn't been my trainin' horse for quite a while. The fella who owned him and sent him to me fer trainin' got so busy with his business and his new girlfriend that he kinda forgot to pay me for a couple of months. By the time he got around to contactin' me, he owed me more in boardin' and trainin' fees than what he was willin' to pay. So he signed Freckles' papers over to me. Freckles has been my horse since early spring. Now he's yours. Or he will be if you'll be so kind as to pick up that pen and print your name in the little blocks."

"Go ahead, Meghan," Mom said. "You earned enough money off the sale of Savannah to buy Freckles."

"If you want him," said Dad.

"Want him?" I nearly shouted. "I love that horse!"

"And he's big enough for you," said Ben. "You two are goin' to be an amazin' team."

About the Author

After earning her teaching degree at Penn State University, Susan Carpenter Noble tucked it in her hip pocket and took off for Colorado to become a horse trainer. Somehow, her mentors got the gangly six-footer to where she could actually get something done on a horse, and she won state championships in such diverse events as Reining, Western Riding, and Working Hunter, on her Quarter Horse, Royal Hank Freckles. She also coached students to state championships in Dressage, Trail, and Barrel Racing, among others.

When she's not out in the arena teaching her Horse Kids, or hiking with her husband, or traveling to see her far-flung siblings and adult kids, she's usually typing away on the keyboard, telling the kinds of horse stories she would like to have read growing up.

Her debut novel, *Cowgirls Don't Quit,* and the sequel, *The Free Horse,* were inspired by two of her recent students. The rest of her students are currently on their best behavior for fear she will embarrass them in a similar manner.

CPSIA information can be obtained
at www.ICGtesting.com
Printed in the USA
LVHW050922120920
665730LV00003B/3